THE ESKIMO'S SECRET

YA
Ke   Keene, Carolyn
       The eskimo's secret.
       #76

DATE DUE

NANCY DREW MYSTERY STORIES®

THE ESKIMO'S SECRET
by
Carolyn Keene

Wanderer Books
Published by Simon & Schuster, Inc., New York

Manufactured in the United States of America
10 9 8 7 6 5 4 3 2 1

NANCY DREW and NANCY DREW MYSTERY STORIES
are trademarks of Simon & Schuster, Inc.
registered in the United States Patent
and Trademark Office

WANDERER and colophon are registered trademarks
of Simon & Schuster, Inc.

Library of Congress Cataloging in Publication Data

Keene, Carolyn.
The Eskimo's secret.

(Nancy Drew mystery stories ; 76)
Summary: Nancy suspects that sabotage in a chain of
West Coast shops selling imported art objects is connected
with the theft of a valuable Eskimo sculpture.
1. Children's stories, American. [1. Mystery and
detective stories] I. Title. II. Series: Keene, Carolyn.
Nancy Drew mystery stories ; 76.
PZ7.K23Nan no. 76   [Fic]   84-20936
ISBN 0-671-55047-0
ISBN 0-671-55046-2 (pbk.)

Contents

1

Imported Problems

"This assignment is a tough one, Dad," eighteen-year-old Nancy Drew told her father over the telephone. "I just can't seem to find anything listed for C-B, Inc."

"I'm not surprised," Carson Drew replied. "I've been trying to get information on Investors, Inc., and I haven't done much better. Obviously, C-B, Inc. and Investors, Inc. are phony corporations. Probably a front for something or someone, so we'll have to do a lot of digging to uncover the real identities."

"Do you want me to give up on C-B, Inc.?" Nancy asked.

"You might as well. Come on back to the hotel and we'll have an early lunch. Maybe we can think of a new approach."

The girl detective, who was only three when her mother died, had a close relationship with her father. A prominent attorney in their home town of River Heights, Mr. Drew frequently called upon Nancy to help him investigate particularly difficult cases all over the country.

"I'll meet you in the dining room," Nancy said as she hung up the phone.

As she headed for the rental car she had picked up at the Seattle, Washington airport, she thought of Helen Haggler's first urgent call to Carson Drew. She was the head of Haggler International Imports, a chain of very elegant shops that sold imported art objects in all the major West Coast cities.

Miss Haggler told Mr. Drew that several unexplained accidents had occurred at the stores recently, and she believed them to be the work of some unknown enemy. She also mentioned receiving several calls from two companies interested in buying her business, but she had dismissed them. One was C-B, Inc. and the other was Investors, Inc. Since she wasn't considering selling her business to them, she had not paid attention to the offers. Now, Miss Haggler wondered if these companies might be responsible for her recent troubles.

When Nancy finally joined her father at a corner table overlooking the bustling city, she asked, a bit teasingly, "Have you decided how we should begin our new approach?"

"At the beginning," Carson Drew responded with a grin. "I think we'll have to trace the owners of every corporation listed in Investors, Inc. I'm sure a lot of them are fakes, but one of them will be the actual people behind Investors, Inc., and that's the one we have to find."

"Then you do think Miss Haggler was right about all the accidents and bad luck she's had being part of a conspiracy?" Nancy asked.

Her father nodded. "Helen isn't the type to get upset over accidents. Our problem is finding out who is to blame for her trouble and getting the proof necessary to turn it over to the police."

"These companies look like they're candidates since they've offered to buy her company," Nancy mused after they'd ordered lunch. "And the fact that we haven't been able to find any real people behind these corporations seems suspicious."

"I've never seen such a paper trail," Carson Drew agreed. "The closest I've come to finding real directors are the names R.K. Smith and D.W. Jones, and that discovery was three corporations removed from Investors, Inc. I haven't been able to locate either of them, so I'm not sure they actually exist."

"Maybe we should be investigating the things that happened to Miss Haggler," Nancy suggested. "Solving a simple case of arson or theft, or even art fraud, would be a snap compared with this."

"I don't think the police would appreciate your attitude," Mr. Drew observed with a chuckle. "They're working on the cases in the cities where there was trouble, but they haven't had much luck so far."

"So what are we going to do?" Nancy asked.

"I think you should call your friend in Victoria," Carson Drew answered. "Perhaps she'd like to come to Seattle and spend a few days with you."

"Are you taking me off this investigation, Dad?" Nancy asked, suddenly troubled.

"Heavens, no, just giving you a brief vacation while I do some very dull digging into the background of Investors, Inc. Maybe I'll pick up something on C-B, Inc. along the way." He frowned. "I thought you'd planned to see Alana."

Nancy picked up her fork and started on her omelette before speaking. Alana Steele was an old friend who had grown up in River Heights.

She'd been orphaned as the result of a tragic car accident several years earlier and had gone to live in Victoria, British Columbia, with her uncle, Clement Steele. She and Nancy had kept in touch with letters and phone calls, but they had not seen each other since Alana left River Heights.

"Of course I want to see her," Nancy said. "I just don't want to neglect you and Miss Haggler."

"There isn't much you can do until I get the real names of the people behind Investors, Inc.," her father assured her.

"Then I'll call her after we finish lunch," Nancy promised. "Now, did you get the report from the San Francisco people?"

"Helen has been cleared of the recent fraud charges made by one of her clients," Mr. Drew reported. "The papers on that jade carving were forged by an unscrupulous dealer. Helen had checked it out properly before offering it to her client, and everything appeared quite correct. The dealer was using her good reputation. The mystery is why the forgery was revealed."

"Another attempt to hurt the reputation of Haggler Imports?" Nancy suggested.

"I can think of no other reason," Carson Drew agreed. "That charge was the final straw. It

11

made me sure that Helen was right about all this trouble being more than just a run of bad luck."

"But why would someone be so eager to buy out her company?" Nancy asked. "I know she's very successful and has possibilities to expand her business beyond the West Coast, but wouldn't all that change if her reputation was ruined?"

Her father nodded.

"Then . . . " Nancy paused. "Could they be doing that to lower the price of the company?" she asked.

Her father considered, then smiled. "You just might be on to something," he admitted.

"And Investors, Inc. must be involved." Nancy frowned.

"That's something you can be thinking about while you're entertaining Alana," her father said.

"That sounds like my cue to go upstairs and make my call," Nancy said.

"Give my regards to her uncle," Carson said.

"Do you know Clement Steele?" Nancy was surprised.

"We've met several times. He's an art dealer, you know, and has quite a nice gallery in Victoria. I believe he specializes in native art—Indian and Eskimo."

"That sounds fascinating," Nancy murmured.

"I suppose that's why Alana has been so interested in studying art these past few years."

"You'll have to ask her about it."

"Talk to you later," Nancy said, getting to her feet.

It took several minutes to place the call to Victoria, but Alana was soon on the phone, her voice full of excitement. "Oh, Nancy, I'm so glad you called," she said. "When I got your letter saying you were going to be in the area, I was happy we'd probably have a chance to talk."

"Well, I'm going to be in Seattle for some time, so I was hoping that you'd be able to come and visit," Nancy invited, giving Alana the details of where she was staying. "I've been helping my father with a case, but he's told me I should take time off. We could do some shopping and sightseeing, if you're free."

There was a long interval of silence. Nancy could hear Alana's breathing on the other end, but nothing else. She waited and waited, a puzzled frown touching her forehead. Finally, she could stand it no longer. "Is this a bad time, Alana?" she asked.

"No, of course not," Alana answered too quickly. "It's just that . . . Nancy, I really can't talk right at the moment. I'll have to call you back. Do you mind?"

"No, I—" Nancy stopped, realizing she was

talking to herself, since the phone on the other end had been disconnected. Her face grew tense as she wondered what was troubling her friend. She replaced the receiver and got up to pace the room.

Time inched by. A half hour passed, then an hour. Finally Nancy could stand it no longer. She dialed the number of the Steele home a second time. It rang and rang unanswered.

Another hour passed and Nancy tried again. This time the housekeeper answered almost at once.

"May I speak with Alana, please," Nancy said, identifying herself.

"I'm sorry, Miss Drew, but Alana is no longer in the house," the housekeeper replied.

"Do you know where I can reach her?" Nancy asked, relieved to think that Alana had not called because she had left the house for some reason.

"She didn't say, Miss. Perhaps you should try the gallery. Mr. Steele might know. Do you wish that number?"

"Please." Nancy wrote down the number, then dialed it at once. The response at the gallery was no more satisfying than the call to Alana's home had been. Unable to accept Alana's prolonged absence, Nancy asked to speak to Mr. Steele.

"I'm sorry to disturb you, sir," she began once she'd introduced herself and told him about her earlier calls. "I'm a little concerned about Alana. It's been two hours since I talked to her and—"

"I can understand your feelings, Nancy," Mr. Steele interrupted. "I've been quite disturbed by Alana's behavior myself. She's been troubled recently and I don't know why. I just hope you'll be able to help her."

"If I can't talk to her, I don't see how I can help," Nancy admitted.

"I simply don't know where she is, Nancy, I'm sorry. As soon as I see her or hear from her, I will insist she return your call, I promise."

"I don't want to put any pressure on her," Nancy murmured. "I'm just worried. She sounded so glad to hear from me and anxious to visit and then . . . nothing."

"I understand. I'm very worried, too." Mr. Steele's voice echoed her anxiety and when she replaced the receiver, Nancy had the chilling feeling that there was a great deal going on that the man hadn't told her—Alana might even be in some sort of danger.

2

A Cry for Help

The afternoon crept by. Nancy dug out the papers her father had been working on and tried to concentrate on them, but her mind kept wandering back to the phone call she'd made to Alana. Finally in a fit of frustration, she shoved the papers back into their folders and dropped on the couch after flipping on the television.

". . . a news bulletin," the television announcer began. "There has been a spectacular robbery at the Steele Gallery in Victoria."

Nancy gasped, her attention fully caught.

"The latest word is that only one item was taken in the robbery. Missing is the reknowned Eskimo sculpture known as the Tundra, which was due for its first public showing this coming

16

weekend. We were lucky enough to attend a pre-showing and have the following tape of this rare art treasure."

The screen was suddenly filled with a sight so incredible that Nancy was transfixed. The base of the sculpture was formed by a huge piece of driftwood that undulated in rolling hills and deep wooden valleys. The artist had created a world on the wood, filling the tiny indentations of the driftwood with dried plants and grasses so that it even looked like the photographs she'd seen of the vast frozen tundra.

This world, however, was more than emptiness, for the artist had filled it with what looked like hundreds of tiny carvings. An entire herd of caribou, the large North American cousins of the reindeer, moved through the center of the piece; but they were only a part of it. Wolves harried the herd and several bears were on the fringes. There were even humans dotted here and there in the intricate landscape.

The carvings were incomparably lovely, the animals and people so lifelike it was hard to believe they weren't real. Nancy felt almost deprived when the tape ended and the newscaster's face came back on the screen.

"This Eskimo carving, done entirely in ivory, has been something of a mystery to lovers of native art objects and has thus brought a great deal of comment from the art community. To have it stolen on the very eve of its showing—"

There was a stir in the crowd behind the newscaster and he turned. "Mr. Steele, Mr. Steele, do you have any word for us? Was anything besides the Tundra taken in the robbery? Do the authorities have any clues?"

The man staring at the camera was tall, attractive, and very angry; his dark eyes flashed and the well-manicured hands were tightening into fists as he forced a smile. "I'm afraid I have no comment at this time," he said.

"Not even to squelch the rumor that this might have been an inside job?" the newscaster asked.

Nancy gasped and jumped as the telephone interrupted her concentration on the television. Mr. Steele looked very much as though he'd like to hit the newscaster, but he only turned away. Nancy swallowed a sign, turned down the sound and picked up the receiver.

"Nancy? Nancy, is that you?" Alana's voice was high and frantic, her breathing ragged as though she were crying.

"Alana, where have you been?" Nancy asked. "What's wrong? Are you all right?"

"No, no, I'm not. I need help, Nancy. Please,

can you come to Victoria?" The last was a sob.

"Of course I'll come," Nancy assured her. "But what's the matter? Is it the robbery? How can I help you?"

"Just come, please, I—" The connection was broken sharply.

"Oh!" Nancy exploded, dialing the number for the Steele house.

"Steele residence." The voice was that of the housekeeper.

"This is Nancy Drew," Nancy said. "I was just talking to Alana and we were cut off. Is she there?"

"Oh, no, Miss Drew, Alana hasn't returned yet. I'm afraid I have no idea where you can reach her."

"But . . ." Nancy started to protest, then gave her thanks, realizing she had no idea where Alana might have been calling from. She considered calling the gallery, then rejected the idea, aware that it would be a scene of mass confusion after the robbery. She was relieved to hear her father's key in the door.

His greeting was warm, but he quickly asked, "Is something wrong, Nancy? Couldn't you reach Alana?"

Nancy began explaining about her calls, Alana's plea for help, and the robbery. He listened without comment until she'd finished, then shook his head. "That doesn't sound good," he said. "Would you like me to call Jeff Carrington? He's an investigator with the police here in Victoria whose specialty is art theft. He's bound to be involved in the case already."

"Oh, Dad, I'd really appreciate it," Nancy replied. "I just don't know what to do. Alana must be in terrible trouble and I want to help her, but first I have to find her!"

"I'll ask Jeff," her father promised. "He'll know if she was at the gallery when the robbery took place." He smiled. "While I'm doing that, why don't you look over the room service menu and make some decisions about dinner? I assume you'll be wanting to stay here in case Alana calls again."

"Thanks, Dad." Nancy gave her father a quick hug before going to get the menu.

Carson Drew's conversation proved to be a long one, and when he finished his expression was rather grim. "I'm afraid the news isn't good, Nancy," he said.

"What do you mean?"

"The newscaster was correct: The authorities do seem to feel that this was an inside job. Whoever took the Tundra knew just where to find it and had access to the private safe at the Steele Gallery."

"But who . . . ?"

"Jeff couldn't give me any details, but from what he implied, I would guess that suspicion at the moment is being directed at Clement Steele, although several of his employees are also being questioned."

"And Alana?" Nancy was almost afraid to ask.

"Jeff said that she wasn't being questioned. In fact, he was quite sure that she hadn't been at the gallery today. She is, however, on the list of people to be contacted."

"Do you suppose that's why she was so upset?" Nancy asked. "Because of the robbery, I mean."

"Didn't you say she sounded nervous earlier?" her father countered.

Nancy nodded. "She was at home then, and when I called the gallery and talked to Mr. Steele, he didn't know where she was."

They sat in silence for several minutes, then Nancy offered her father the menu, asking his comments before she ordered. They were halfway through dinner when the telephone rang once again. Carson Drew answered it, then handed the receiver to Nancy. "Mr. Steele."

"Hello, Mr. Steele," Nancy said. "Are you calling for Alana?"

"Is she there?" Mr. Steele asked.

"Here? Of course not," Nancy gasped. "I just meant—"

"She's not in Seattle? You haven't talked to her?" Mr. Steele's voice dropped.

"I haven't talked to her since she called and asked me to help her," Nancy began.

"When was that? Was it after we talked?"

"Yes it was. Actually, it was while I was watching the news report about the robbery. That's why I didn't call you at the gallery."

"What exactly did she say?"

Nancy reported the conversation as well as she could remember it, ending, "I promised her I'd come and help, but I don't know where to reach her, Mr. Steele. I tried calling your house again, but they said she hadn't been home."

"She hasn't." His voice was weary.

"Do you know what's wrong?" Nancy asked. "Is it the robbery? I want to help her." The too familiar click stopped her words.

"Is something wrong?" her father asked.

"Mr. Steele just hung up on me," Nancy reported, frustration making her angry. "It seems like everyone I talk to is doing that. Nobody wants to give me any answers."

"Frustrating, isn't it?" Carson Drew observed. "I've been getting a lot of that, too."

"How is the Haggler case going?" Nancy inquired, eager for the change of subject. "I've been so worried about Alana I didn't even ask."

"Like your telephone conversations," Mr. Drew replied. "I've never run into so many dead ends. It's like being in a maze. Everywhere I turn I find a promising lead; I follow it and run directly into a wall."

"Is there anything I can do?" Nancy asked.

"Help me eat this dessert," her father answered. "I ordered too much dinner."

"Didn't I warn you about that?" Nancy teased. "Hannah would never approve."

Her father responded with a story of another multi-course meal and Nancy found herself laughing in spite of her fears for Alana. There seemed to be nothing she could do at the moment, so it was better not to dwell on all the terrible things that might be happening to her friend.

The evening passed slowly. The news was full of reports of the robbery, but it was soon clear that no one knew any more than they had during the first moment when Nancy had seen the news flash. Still, Nancy enjoyed watching the reports because they showed the short tape of the Tundra sculpture and she found it hypnotizing.

About halfway through the evening the telephone rang again. Nancy raced to answer it, then suppressed her disappointment when she recognized Helen Haggler's voice. "May I speak with Carson, Nancy?" the woman asked.

"Of course, Miss Haggler, just a moment." Nancy handed her father the receiver, which caused him to raise an eyebrow.

Nancy returned to the television, but even as she watched, she was conscious of her father's voice and the change in his tone. He was upset, she could tell, and he was frowning when he finally replaced the receiver.

"Is something wrong, Dad?" Nancy asked.

"I'm not sure," he replied.

"Was Miss Haggler unhappy with our progress?"

"She didn't even ask." Carson Drew sighed. "She called to tell me she wants the investigation of Investors, Inc. stopped," he explained. "And she refuses to tell me why."

"Stopped, but I thought . . . ?" Nancy let it trail off. "What are you going to do?" she asked sure her father wasn't going to be so easily put off.

24

"I'm going out to her estate first thing in the morning," Carson said.

"Do you think someone has threatened her?" Nancy asked, following his line of thought without any difficulty.

"Knowing Helen Haggler, I doubt she'd give in to simple threats. She didn't get where she is today without being a very strong lady."

"Then what?"

"I don't know, but I'm going to find out. I'm not going to stop my investigation until I know exactly what has changed her mind." His face was set and hard and Nancy felt a sudden chill of fear for him.

"Do you want me to go with you?" she asked, almost timidly.

"You'd better stay here and try to reach Alana," he said.

Nancy nodded, but the premonition of disaster didn't go away.

3

Strange Disappearance

Carson Drew left for the Haggler estate early the next morning; by eight o'clock, Nancy was pacing the floor. Unable to wait any longer for Alana's call, she tried the Steele mansion once again. The housekeeper answered in an already weary tone.

"May I speak with Alana?" Nancy asked, then identified herself, sure that the household had been bombarded by calls from reporters.

"I'm sorry, Miss Drew, but Miss Steele is away," the housekeeper responded.

"Away?" Nancy frowned. "But I don't understand."

"She left on a trip around lunchtime yesterday, Miss. I'm very sorry." The connection was broken before Nancy could protest.

"Away on a trip, my foot," Nancy murmured to herself, suddenly sure her friend was in real trouble. "If she left, it wasn't on anything as casual as a little trip."

Nancy spent a few minutes reviewing all that had happened since yesterday's call to Alana, and none of it made much sense to her. She was haunted by the call from Alana and her plea for help.

"There's no use waiting around here," she told herself firmly. Her father would be gone most of the day, and perhaps even overnight if his conference with Miss Haggler continued late into the day. Alana had begged her to come and help, and Nancy, sure that help was needed, was ready to go.

Packing an overnight case and calling about arrangements to get from Seattle to Victoria didn't take very long. She felt better as soon as she was on her way. She only hoped her father wouldn't be too upset to come back to the hotel and find only a note waiting for him.

Once in Victoria, Nancy hesitated. She considered calling the Steele mansion again, but she had a strong suspicion that she would only be told the same story. Better to rent a car and just drive to the mansion.

Nancy arrived there a little before noon. A maid answered her knock, but would tell her only that neither Alana nor Mr. Steele was at home. When Nancy requested more information, the maid summoned the housekeeper, whom she called Mrs. Dentley. The housekeeper merely repeated the story she'd given Nancy on the telephone.

"Alana asked me to come," Nancy protested, sensing that the woman was lying. "I really must see her."

The woman shrugged and closed the door on Nancy, leaving her standing on the doorstep.

Frustrated, Nancy looked around. The estate was set well back from the street in the midst of beautifully cared for gardens. Flower scents filled the air and in the distance she could hear the steady whirring of a mower.

Aware that pounding on the door would bring her no information, Nancy followed the sound of the mower around to the side of the mansion. A young man was operating it, and he stopped at once when he saw her.

"May I help you?" he asked.

"I've come to see Alana Steele," Nancy said, liking his friendly grin. "She called me yesterday and asked me to come and help her, but now she doesn't seem to be home and I don't know where to get in touch with her. Do you have any idea where she might be?"

The young man studied her for a moment, then shrugged. "She left the house shortly after noon yesterday. I noticed, because she ran out like someone was after her. Hopped in her car and took off. As far as I know, she hasn't come back."

"Not even last night?" Nancy's worry about her friend deepened.

"Her car is kind of noisy and I live over the garage, so I would have heard it if she'd come in."

"Did she take any luggage with her?" Nancy asked, remembering the housekeeper's story about a trip.

The young man shook his head. "Mr. Steele might know where she is," he suggested. "Or maybe her boyfriend would."

"Who would that be?" Nancy inquired.

"Tod Harper. He works with her at the gallery."

Nancy sighed, sure that she'd gotten all the information she could from the young man, and feeling even more anxious about Alana. She thanked him and returned to her car. It was obvious that the Steele Gallery would have to be her next stop and she was sure she wasn't going to find Alana there. She only hoped that Alana's uncle would have more information for her today than he'd had last night.

The Steele Gallery was a handsome building, new but carefully designed to fit in with the older structures on each side. At the moment, however, it boasted a large CLOSED sign on the front door and there were several official-looking cars parked in the area. Not sure she would be admitted, Nancy tried the front door. To her surprise, it was unlocked.

"We're closed today, Miss." The guard stepped out of the shadows the moment she entered the dim reception area.

"I was looking for Mr. Steele or Tod Harper," Nancy said quickly. "I'm a friend of Alana Steele's."

The man's eyes remained unfriendly as he studied her for a moment, then he nodded. "You will find them both down that hall to your left."

Nancy took two steps in the indicated direction.

"Wait a minute," the guard said. "You're not a reporter or anything, are you?" he asked.

"No, I'm not," Nancy answered.

"Better not be," the guard muttered as he waved her forward. "They aren't giving any interviews today, that's for sure."

Nancy followed the hall to where a series of offices lined a corridor behind the main showrooms of the gallery. Since only one office bore a name—"Clement Steele"—Nancy headed for it.

"I don't have to listen to this!" The man's voice was loud and full of anger, stopping Nancy's hand before she could knock on the door.

"You work for me; you'll listen to whatever I have to say," an equally angry voice replied.

Nancy took a step back, ready to retreat to the guard station and perhaps ask to use the phone there to call Mr. Steele's office. However, before she could turn away, the argument grew more interesting.

"I came to ask about Alana," the first voice said.

"I'd like to know about my niece, too." The second voice was obviously that of Clement Steele. "Suppose you tell me where she is, Harper."

"Mr. Steele, I don't know." Tod Harper sounded miserable. "I haven't seen her since the night before last. I don't know why you think I have."

"I blame you for all of this, Harper," Mr. Steele growled.

"For the theft?" Harper was obviously surprised. "I wasn't even in the building, you know that."

"Well, I'm sure it wasn't Alana's doing, no matter what the authorities think." Mr. Steele sounded more worried than angry now.

"They only want to talk to her," Harper protested. "If she'd tell them where she was yesterday, they'd know she didn't have anything to do with the theft of the Tundra."

Nancy gasped at this proof that the worst of her fears had been realized. She agreed with the men that Alana could have had no part in the art theft, but her disappearance at the same time did seem very suspicious.

"And who told them she was gone?" Clement Steele demanded. "And spent half the night telling anyone who would listen that Alana was obsessed with the carving?"

"I had to answer their questions," Tod Harper stated.

"You had to give them someone else to suspect," Steele snapped.

"Just as you did when you sent them around to question me," Harper accused. "I don't have the combination to the gallery safe, but *you* do."

"I know *I* didn't give you the combination," Steele corrected. "But that doesn't mean you don't have it. Alana could have told you."

"You'd rather have them suspect Alana than you, wouldn't you?" Tod Harper shouted. "Why is that? Are you afraid they'll find out that you stole the Tundra yourself?"

"I don't have to listen to your half-baked theories," Clement Steele thundered. "You're fired! I only kept you on because Alana liked you."

The door of the office exploded open with a crash and Nancy was nearly run over by the stocky blond young man who came through it. He passed her without a glance and Nancy turned to face the angry stare of the man in the doorway.

"Who are you and what do you think you're doing eavesdropping outside my office?" Clement Steele demanded, his eyes blazing with fury.

4

Several Suspects

"I'm Nancy Drew, Mr. Steele," Nancy said, holding herself very still and straight so he wouldn't know she was a bit frightened of him.

"Nancy, my dear girl, I should have recognized you from Alana's photos. I'm sorry. Do come in, please."

Nancy stepped into his office with relief, glad of an opportunity to talk to Alana's uncle in private. His overly friendly greeting rather surprised her, as did the frown he turned her way after she was seated in front of his desk.

"What brings you to Victoria, Nancy?" he asked.

"Alana's call," Nancy answered.

"Has she called you again?" Mr. Steele sat forward, his body tense.

"Not since I talked to you," Nancy admitted, "but as I told you, she begged me to come here and help her. When I couldn't reach her again, I decided I had to come in person and try to find out what was wrong."

Mr. Steele sighed and leaned back in his chair, suddenly looking much older and wearier than he had a moment before. "I hope you don't regret your decision," he said.

"Regret it?" Nancy frowned. "Why should I? I don't understand."

"Alana isn't here," he explained. "I have no idea where she is."

"When I went by your home the housekeeper told me that Alana left on a trip," Nancy told him, watching him closely.

Mr. Steele winced. "She did leave yesterday," he stated emphatically.

"After she talked to me—and without taking any luggage," Nancy added.

"I asked Mrs. Dentley to lie," Mr. Steele admitted. "The authorities have been asking a lot of questions about Alana and so have the reporters. They seem determined to make some sort of connection between Alana's departure and the theft. I'm hoping that the statement that she left *before* the theft will force them to look elsewhere for a suspect."

"You're just trying to protect her?" Nancy couldn't help being skeptical after having overheard the argument between him and Tod Harper.

"Until I can find out where she is and why she left, I've got to do something." Although his concern seemed genuine, Nancy had a strong feeling he was not being completely truthful.

"What about the theft?" Nancy asked. "Have the authorities told you anything about it?"

Mr. Steele was on his feet at once. "They ask a lot of questions, but they don't answer many," he said grimly.

"Was the Tundra the only thing taken?" Nancy wasn't sure what approach to take in her questioning.

"A masterpiece beyond compare. The most exciting exhibit I've ever been offered and now it's gone. The theft will ruin me, whether or not I'm cleared of suspicion. Who'd want to trust anything to my gallery after this?"

"When the thieves are caught—" Nancy began, but Mr. Steele was already on his way to the door.

"I'm sorry I can't help you any further, Nancy," he said, "but I really have no idea where she is. I will call you if I hear anything."

Reluctantly, Nancy got to her feet and left the

office. She looked around hoping for inspiration, but no new path of investigation opened in the quiet hall, so she headed back the way she'd come. Since she was curious about the rest of the pieces that were to be displayed with the Tundra, she turned down a side hall. As she hoped, it led directly to the showroom.

Natural light from the gallery windows spilled over the room. The central enclosed pedestal was empty, but the other displays were intriguing. Nancy crossed to the first one.

"They really aren't much without the Tundra," a slightly familiar voice said.

Nancy whirled to see Tod Harper standing near a collection of polar bear carvings. "What are you doing here?" she demanded.

"I could ask you the same question," he replied with a slight grin, "but the truth is, I've been waiting for you."

"How did you know I'd come in here?"

"Alana told me how interested you are in mysteries and I figured you couldn't resist this one." The grin became engaging, warming his blue eyes and making him a very attractive young man. "You did come, Nancy Drew."

Nancy giggled, a little embarrassed by her own suspicions. "So I did," she admitted. Why did you want to see me?"

"To ask you to help Alana. That *is* why you're here, isn't it? You won't let Clement Steele send you away?" The grin was gone. "He's hiding something and it could hurt Alana."

"How did you know who I am?" Nancy asked, suddenly aware she'd learned his identity by eavesdropping and wondering if he might have done the same thing.

"Alana has a couple of pictures of you," Tod answered, "and she talks about you quite a bit. Besides, I've read about you in the papers when you've solved mysteries for people." He sighed. "I just want you to solve this one."

"What do you know about Alana's disappearance?" Nancy asked, accepting his explanation.

"Nothing. We had a date the night before last, but it was just ordinary—dinner and a movie. I've gone over the whole evening in my mind a hundred times." He sighed. "I called her yesterday afternoon, but I didn't reach her. I didn't realize she was missing until the authorities started asking me a lot of questions about her."

"Then you have no idea where she could have gone?" Nancy asked, frustrated at not getting any useful information.

"None whatsoever. Do you?"

After a moment of consideration, Nancy told Tod about the phone calls, including Alana's

38

plea for help. He looked as disturbed as she felt. "She was worried about something before the theft," Nancy finished, "and she was frantic afterward."

"Then you think the two things are connected?" Tod didn't sound happy about the idea.

"I think they must be," Nancy said. "But I'm sure Alana didn't steal the sculpture."

"So am I."

"What can you tell me about the sculpture?" Nancy asked. "And about the owner?"

"Almost nothing," Tod replied. "I mean, I can tell you about the carvings themselves, that sort of thing, but that's not what you want, is it?"

Nancy shook her head. "What I . . . " She stopped speaking when Tod stiffened. She turned to follow his gaze and saw that Mr. Steele was standing in the doorway behind her.

"Ah, so here you are, Nancy," he said with a joviality that didn't reach his eyes. "I asked the guard if you'd left the building and he told me you hadn't."

"Was there something you wanted?" Nancy asked, aware that he was looking past her at Tod Harper and his glare was furious.

"Please come back to my office," he invited, his gesture drawing her away from Tod and into the hall behind him. "Out of the building, Harper," Mr. Steele growled. "You're not welcome here."

"Leaving will be a pleasure," Tod snapped, going the other way.

Mr. Steele said nothing until they'd returned to his office. "I'm sorry to interrupt your conversation, but I've been thinking I would very much like to have you stay in Victoria and try to find Alana."

"You want me to stay?" Nancy couldn't hide her surprise.

"I'm terribly worried, Nancy. Alana was trying to reach you, so I'm sure she wants your help. If you would be my guest at the house, perhaps she'll try to reach you there. I just hope it's soon."

"You think her disappearance is connected with the theft, don't you?" Nancy asked.

"I don't think she stole it, if that's what you mean." His face was grim.

"Neither do I," Nancy assured him, "but she might have seen something or heard something that told her who did take it. If she knew too much . . . " She didn't want to finish the thought.

"Then you have to find her quickly."

"I'll need some help," Nancy said, pleased at

his change of attitude.

"Anything."

"Tell me about the Tundra," Nancy requested. "Who owns it? Who would want to steal it?"

"The Tundra was the masterpiece of a private collection originally belonging to Franklin Cole. He died about six months ago and his wife offered me the collection. While alive, Mr. Cole never displayed the sculpture, but after his death his wife was harrassed by a number of very insistent buyers and she couldn't stand the pressure. She felt that hiding such a monumental work of art in a private collection was wrong and she intimated that she would allow me to handle the sale of it to someone or some institution that would display it permanently as the valuable part of the Eskimo heritage she feels it to be." Mr. Steele spoke with calm authority on the subject, but his expression was sad. "It seems she trusted the wrong person," he finished.

"Do you think the theft was done by one of those buyers?" Nancy asked.

He nodded.

"But I thought the authorities said it was an inside job," Nancy protested.

"There was inside help," he confirmed. "Will

you stay on, Nancy? Try to find Alana?"

"Of course." Nancy made her decision.

"I'll call Mrs. Dentley and tell her to expect you." Mr. Steele looked relieved.

"Would it be all right if I talked to some of the people here at the gallery?" Nancy asked.

"Of course. If anyone is reluctant to answer your questions, just let me know."

"I'll contact you as soon as I learn anything," Nancy assured him, hoping it wouldn't be long.

The next hour was discouraging. Questioning the employees of the gallery proved frustrating, for everyone seemed to agree that Alana was obsessed with the Tundra, but no one could tell her why. Nor did any of them offer suggestions about other people she might talk to. Nancy finally went to the receptionist's desk, hoping the woman would be able to give her names and addresses of other people who'd worked at the gallery, people that might know Alana better than the ones she'd talked to.

"Miss Nancy Drew?" A young boy called out as he came in the front door.

"I'm Nancy Drew," Nancy confirmed.

He stepped forward and handed her an envelope. Nancy looked at it, seeking a return address, her thoughts on her father. There was none. She began tearing it open.

The note was typed on a single sheet of paper.

Nancy Drew,
Give up your search and leave Victoria. Alana will not be found and you are in danger. 'A Friend'

5

A Friend in Hiding

Nancy gasped, then looked around for the boy who'd brought the envelope; but he had vanished.

"What is it?" the receptionist asked.

Nancy handed her the note, then ran to the front door to peer out into the street, hoping to catch a glimpse of the boy. He was nowhere to be seen. She returned to the receptionist's desk with a frown.

"Would you like me to call the authorities?" the woman asked as Nancy reclaimed the note.

Nancy considered, then shook her head. "I'm sure it's just a prank," she said.

The receptionist's expression told her the woman didn't believe it.

"I'd appreciate it if you didn't mention this to

anyone," Nancy continued. "Mr. Steele has asked me to stay at his home to wait for Alana, so I'll be perfectly safe. However, I would like Tod Harper's home address and phone number, as well as the names of the two employees that left the gallery earlier this year."

The receptionist dug out the information while Nancy studied the note and the envelope more thoroughly. It was obvious the messenger had not been working for a regular delivery firm. Since Tod Harper was the only person besides Mr. Steele to know why she was in Victoria, it seemed likely he had sent the warning. What bothered her was why?

Nancy took the information and left the gallery, seeking a public telephone for her calls. The first was to Seattle, for she was anxious to know how her father had fared with Miss Haggler and to tell him what had been happening here.

"Mr. Drew has not returned to the hotel, Miss Drew," the desk clerk reported. "There are several messages for him."

"Are there any for me?" Nancy asked.

"I'm afraid not," was the answer. "Did you wish to leave a message?"

"Just a note telling my father that I can be reached at the Steele home," Nancy said after a moment of thought. She wasn't sure her father would approve of her staying on in Victoria to search for Alana; but she didn't want to return to Seattle to discuss it. Time might be very important if Alana was in danger.

She tried the other numbers she'd gotten from the receptionist, without much luck. No one answered any of them. Feeling frustrated, she drove to the Steele mansion again, this time to be welcomed warmly by Mrs. Dentley.

Once she was settled in the guest room, Nancy asked the maid to show her to Alana's room, which was just down the hall. Though she felt like an intruder, it was the only place she could think of to look for clues to her friend's disappearance. She began searching the rather untidy area.

Books and papers were everywhere, making clear just how deeply interested Alana was in Eskimo art and in ivory carving. Nancy checked them carefully, seeking references to the Tundra, hoping for information on the owner and the history of the piece; but she found nothing. Frustrated, she sat down at Alana's desk.

"Where have you gone, Alana?" she asked the pretty, feminine room. "Why didn't you leave me one clue?"

She tried to pick up the corner of the blotter that protected the fine wood of the desk and gasped as a small ivory polar bear tumbled off the desk and bounced under the four-poster bed. Nancy dropped to her knees and felt under the heavy rose satin of the bedspread. Her fingers found nothing.

"Now where did you go?" she murmured, lifting the thick fabric so a little light could spill under the bed. For a moment, she saw nothing, then a vague shadow caught her eye and she lay down on the thick carpet to peer under the bed at a better angle.

It wasn't hard to spot the bear, but when she reached for it, she felt the tickling of something hanging down from the bedsprings. Investigating, she found a trailing piece of tape leading up to what looked like a small cardboard box lid.

"What in the world?" she asked, prying the lid loose from the rest of the tape that secured it to the bedsprings. A small notebook dropped from the box lid into her hand.

Reaching for the bear, Nancy brought both articles to the desk. She put the bear back where she'd found it, then turned her attention to the notebook. It was a very ordinary small looseleaf notebook, but the single word inked on the cover told her why it had been hidden away. It was titled "Tundra" in Alana's distinctive handwriting.

Nancy was just ready to open the book when there was a light knock on the door. "Miss Drew?" The maid peered in.

"What is it?" Nancy asked, covering the notebook with some of Alana's papers.

"You have a phone call, Miss Drew," the girl answered.

"My father?" Nancy wondered hopefully.

"The gentleman didn't give his name," the maid replied. "If you'd like to come down to the library?"

"I'll be right with you," Nancy said. "I just want to put things back the way they were." She stood up, moving her body between the desk and the maid and carefully putting the notebook in her pocket. It made a slight bulge, but it was better than leaving it behind, she decided.

"Did you find out where Miss Alana is?" the girl asked as Nancy followed her out into the upstairs hall.

Nancy sighed. "I'm afraid not," she admitted. "Do you happen to know of anyone I could call? A girlfriend she was close to?"

The girl shook her head, then hurried down

the stairs to open the door of the handsome library. "You can take the call here," she said.

Nancy smiled and thanked her, then waited until the girl had closed the door behind her before picking up the receiver. "Hello," she said.

"Nancy, are you really there?" Alana's voice was breathless, high.

"Alana? Where *are* you?" Nancy's heart leaped with relief.

"That doesn't matter," Alana answered. "What are you doing in Victoria?"

"I came to help you," Nancy replied, surprised by her friend's tone. "You asked me to, remember."

"You shouldn't have come."

"Your uncle is frantic with worry and so is Tod," Nancy told her. "They both asked me to try to find you. You have to come home, Alana. The authorities think you stole the Tundra."

"I don't have it." The words were almost a sob.

"I know that and so does your uncle, but until you talk to the officers in charge of the investigation, you'll be a suspect, Alana. Why did you run away? Where are you?"

"I can't tell you." Alana's voice was sad, but firm.

"How can I help you if you won't talk to me?" Nancy demanded, her frustration growing with her fear that Alana might hang up the phone. "Dont you trust me, Alana?"

"No one can help me now. It's too late."

"It can't be too late," Nancy snapped. "You called me, Alana. Now give me a chance. Just tell me where you are.

"No, no you can't find me. It's too late. You have to leave Victoria, Nancy. Go back to Seattle before you get hurt. I found the secret of the Tundra at the Firebird and now I . . . Please, Nancy, just go before you learn too much!"

6

A Ransacked Room

The phone clicked dead in her ear and Nancy nearly screamed in frustration. Why did people keep hanging up on her? All she wanted to do was help. She closed her eyes and tried to remember everything that Alana had said, hoping it would somehow start to make sense, but it didn't.

Not sure what to do next, Nancy dialed Tod Harper's number again, not really expecting an answer. She was anxious to talk to someone, anyone, about Alana's mysterious call. To her surprise, Tod answered on the first ring.

"Well, what can I do for you?" he asked cheerfully when Nancy identified herself.

"I'd like to talk to you about Alana," Nancy said.

51

"Have you heard from her again?" Tod inquired, his tone changing.

"Yes, I—"

"Not on the phone," Tod said, cutting her off.

"Do you want to come here?" Nancy asked, not sure what his caution meant.

"No. I think we should meet somewhere else." Tod sounded troubled.

"Where?"

"How about the Inner Harbour near the Empress Hotel? You know where that is, don't you?"

"Of course."

"We could talk safely on one of those horse-drawn sightseeing rides," Tod continued. He suggested they meet there in half an hour, then he hung up.

Nancy replaced the receiver of the library telephone, then stood looking at nothing for a moment. What was Tod afraid of? Was he somehow involved in Alana's disappearance? Or was it that he thought Mr. Steele was involved? She hadn't a clue and it bothered her.

Nancy slipped her hand into her pocket, her fingers lightly caressing the notebook. For a moment she wished she hadn't called Tod, hadn't agreed to meet him. She longed for time to look into the notebook to see what it was Alana had hidden so carefully. Then the memories of the panic in Alana's voice swept over her and she knew she had to do more than read the notebook. Alana was in trouble or danger and she needed help!

Mrs. Dentley was just coming out of the dining room when Nancy left the library. "Is everything satisfactory?" she asked with a smile.

"Everything is fine, thank you," Nancy assured her. "I'll be going out for an hour or two now. If my father calls, tell him I'll call him back as soon as I return."

"I'll be happy to." Mrs. Dentley's smile faded. "I do hope you find Alana," she said.

"I'll do my best," Nancy assured her, feeling guilty about not telling her of the phone call she'd just received. She hurried up to the guest room to get her purse, taking time only to tuck the notebook into it before she left.

The streets of Victoria were pretty but busy, and once she found the spot Tod had mentioned, she rather enjoyed the wait. Small flower baskets hung from old-fashioned lampposts, and clusters of geraniums and petunias added bright spots of color as she looked across the street to where the ivy-draped Empress Hotel stood. A tourist wagon passed and Nancy glanced at her watch. Tod was late. Frowning, she went to a telephone to call him.

There was no answer at his apartment, so she

returned to the meeting place. When a second horse-drawn wagon passed, Nancy felt an icy chill of premonition. Tod Harper tricked me, she thought angrily.

She tried his apartment once more, then drove back to the Steele mansion. Her suspicions of trouble were confirmed when the front door was opened by a man in uniform.

"Nancy, where in the world have you been?" Mr. Steele asked as he emerged from the library, his face dark with anger.

"I went out to meet Tod Harper," Nancy said, aware that she wasn't going to make him any happier.

"What did he want?" Mr. Steele demanded. "You should have known better than to trust him."

Nancy agreed, glumly. She looked around, noting more men moving purposefully through the halls of the mansion. "Did something happen here while I was away?"

"I'm afraid so," said the man who'd admitted her, before Mr. Steele could answer. "Are you Nancy Drew?"

"Yes, I am," Nancy said, her heart sinking.

"Would you come upstairs, please, Miss Drew," the man requested. "We'd like you to check your belongings and tell us if anything is missing."

"Missing?"

"Someone broke in, Nancy," Mr. Steele said.

"You mean there was a burglary here?" Nancy asked, not sure she believed her own ears.

"We're not sure that anything was taken," Mr. Steele said. "At least, nothing seems to be missing."

Nancy started to ask for more details, but her host had already turned away and disappeared back into the library, closing the door behind him. Frowning, Nancy followed the uniformed officer upstairs. Since her room was at the far end of the hall, they passed the door of Alana's room on the way.

"The maid said you were in here earlier," the officer said. "Do you think you could tell if anything was missing?"

"From Alana's room?" Nancy began, then gasped as the man opened the door. The room was a shambles. Every drawer had been dumped out, every book tossed from the shelf. Nothing was left as it had been just two hours ago.

"Can you help us?" the officer asked.

Nancy could only shake her head. "I was in the room briefly, but I didn't notice . . . The only items I remember clearly are an ivory polar bear on the corner of the desk and the ornate clock on the dresser, and I see they're still here."

The officer nodded. "So far we haven't found anything obvious that's missing."

"Do you have any idea what they were searching for?" Nancy asked.

He shook his head. They left the mess behind and moved on to her room. Nancy felt sick when she looked inside. She'd brought little with her, but it was obvious that someone had been through everything.

"What would they be looking for among your things?" the officer asked.

Nancy's fingers tightened on her purse, not really able to feel the notebook inside, but aware that it was there. "Whatever they couldn't find in Alana's room," she replied as calmly as she could. Then she asked, "Where were the servants when this was happening?"

"In the kitchen and dining room according to the housekeeper. They were preparing for the evening meal." He smiled. "And there was no sign of forced entry, Miss Drew. Whoever did this either had keys or had help from someone inside the house. Is there anything missing from your things?" he asked after a moment of silence.

Nancy checked quickly, then shook her head.

"Shall we go back down and talk to Mr. Steele?"

Nancy rubbed the edges of her purse again, suddenly sure that the notebook inside was what the thief had been after. But why? What could it hold that would goad someone into such a violent search? She had to give it to the authorities, she realized unhappily, yet she longed to read it first.

"You see what you've done," Mr. Steele growled the moment Nancy stepped into the library.

"I've done? she gasped. "I don't understand what you mean."

"You let him in, didn't you? You called that Tod Harper and let him in so he could search for whatever he wanted."

"But I didn't," Nancy said. "I told you I made an appointment to meet him near the Empress Hotel. He didn't come, but I'm not at all sure he's the one who—"

"He did it all right. He's behind all this. If Alana's in trouble, it's his fault. I never trusted him."

The ringing of the telephone stopped him from saying more. The officer took the call. He spoke softly, then listened, his face grave. When he hung up the receiver, he turned to Nancy. "When did you talk to Tod Harper?" he asked.

Nancy answered easily, for she'd checked her

watch right after promising to meet him. "Why?" she asked.

"Tod Harper is not responsible for what happened here," the officer said quietly. "He didn't keep his appointment with Miss Drew because he was on his way to the hospital."

"What?" Nancy gasped. "Is he all right?"

"He has a concussion and a lot of minor injuries. He was struck by a hit-and-run driver shortly after he left his apartment."

7

The Elusive Detective

"A hit-and-run driver?" Nancy exclaimed. "But . . ."

"Harper was in an accident?" Mr. Steel didn't sound quite convinced.

"He was struck down," the officer said. "But it certainly doesn't sound like it was an accident."

"You mean he was injured on purpose?" Nancy was sickened at the thought, but not surprised.

"There were two witnesses and both of them stated that the car had been parked at the curb with the motor running for some time. When Harper came out of his apartment building, the car pulled out and headed directly for him. According to both witnesses, Harper saw the car and tried to avoid it. The car pursued him, finally striking him just before he reached the far curb."

Nancy shuddered. "How awful."

"He was very lucky to get away with just a concussion and the other cuts and bruises," the officer agreed. Then he turned his attention to Mr. Steele. "Now, sir, I'd like you to explain to me why you were so sure that Tod Harper was the person who ransacked your niece's room."

Nancy started to speak up, but the officer turned to her. "If you'll excuse us, Miss Drew," he said.

Nancy hesitated for a moment, then said, "If you don't mind, Mr. Steele, I'd like to try to reach my father.

"By all means, my dear," he said. "We can talk in the other room. This must have been a terrible shock to you. When I invited you to stay here, I certainly had no idea you would be subjected to something like this."

The men left Nancy alone in the library, closing the door behind them, but she didn't place her call immediately. She needed time to think. Everything had happened so quickly she'd just been reacting. And she needed her father's advice.

She started to pick up the telephone, then felt a twinge of doubt. If the car had been waiting for Tod, that meant the driver had to know he was going out. And whoever had searched the mansion would have to know that she would be gone, too. She suddenly understood why Tod had been so reluctant to discuss anything on the telephone. He must know or suspect that either his phone or this one must be tapped.

Nancy checked the instrument quickly and could find nothing, so she dialed the Seattle hotel again. She would be careful what she said, she decided. All she really needed was to make arrangements to call her father back from a public telephone.

"I'm sorry, Miss Drew," the desk clerk said. "Mr. Drew still hasn't picked up his messages. Do you want me to check yours?"

"Please," Nancy said, feeling frustrated and wondering if she should try to reach her father at the Haggler estate.

"Oh, he did call in for you," the clerk responded cheerfully. "There's a Victoria number for you to call. Do you have a pencil?"

Nancy took down the number and thanked the clerk, then dialed it.

"Creighton Hotel," a friendly voice said.

"Ah . . . Do you have a Carson Drew registered there?" Nancy asked, too surprised to think clearly for a moment.

"Yes, ma'am," the voice answered after a long

pause. "We have a Carson Drew and a Nancy Drew." There was another brief pause, then the voice continued. "We have reservations in those names," he corrected himself. "Neither one has checked in so far. Did you wish to leave a message?"

"This is Nancy Drew," Nancy said. "When were those reservations made?"

"This afternoon. Will you be checking in soon, Miss Drew?"

"Yes, of course. I'll be there in about an hour. If my father arrives before I do, would you please tell him to expect me?" Her confusion gave way to relief at the idea of sitting down with her father and telling him everything that had happened.

Still, after she'd replaced the receiver, she stayed where she was, frowning. Why should her father have come to Victoria? Was it in connection with the Haggler case? And, perhaps more curious, why hadn't he called her to tell her he'd booked rooms? Why leave a message at the hotel in Seattle?

A knock on the door pulled her attention back to her present situation. She got to her feet as Mr. Steele entered. "Did you reach your father, Nancy?" he asked.

"No," Nancy replied. "It seems he's on his

way to Victoria. He's booked rooms for us at the Creighton Hotel."

"Then you won't be staying here?" Mr. Steele didn't look too disturbed.

"You've been very kind, but no. Are the officers still here? I should tell them where I can be reached."

"They just left, but I'll give them the message if they check back tonight."

Nancy thought of the notebook in her purse and felt a twinge of relief. She certainly didn't want to turn it over to Mr. Steele, since she still felt he was hiding something.

"If you'll excuse me, I'll go up and pack my things," she said.

"Would you and your father be my guests for dinner this evening?" Mr. Steele asked, surprising her once again. "It would be a professional consultation, if your father would consider representing me at this time."

"I'm sorry," Nancy said, " but I can't speak for him, Mr. Steele. I'm not even sure when he will be arriving in Victoria. He hadn't reached the hotel yet when I called.

Mr. Steele nodded. "Well, please ask him to call me when you do see him."

"Of course." Nancy started toward the door, suddenly anxious to leave the house.

"It's for Alana's protection," Mr. Steele said, stopping her. "The longer she's missing, the more trouble she's going to face when she returns. The gallery has its lawyers, but I'd like someone special to represent her."

"I'm sure my father would be glad to help her," Nancy said. "The important thing is for us to find her." She hesitated a moment, then told Mr. Steele about the phone call she'd received saying only that Alana had warned her to leave Victoria.

Mr. Steele shook his head. "Perhaps she's right, Nancy," he said. "I have no right to ask you to stay here and put yourself in danger. Until I heard what happened to Harper, I honestly didn't think there was any danger. I'll understand if your father insists on your returning to Seattle tomorrow."

"I'm not going anywhere," Nancy stated, making up her mind. "Alana called here for me because she needs my help, no matter what she said."

"She didn't say where she is?"

Nancy shook her head. "And I don't think she's the one who placed the call," she observed, thinking out loud.

"What do you mean?"

64

"The maid said a gentleman was calling, but when I answered, it was Alana."

"But who would be with her?" Mr. Steele murmured.

"I was planning to ask Tod if he had any ideas," Nancy admitted. "You don't know who it could be, do you?"

Mr. Steele shook his head, but his eyes skittered away from hers guiltily. Finally, she sighed and started for the door again. He said nothing to stop her.

It took little time to pack her few belongings, though she had to check the room carefully since everything had been torn apart by whoever was looking for the notebook. She would be glad to leave, yet she felt she was deserting Alana, since her friend would have no idea where to reach her now.

After leaving the Creighton Hotel number with Mr. Steele and the servants, she set off alone. As she drove across town to the hotel, Nancy realized how famished she was, after her whirlwind day. She hurried into the respectable old hotel, eager to see her father, to sit down to dinner with him and discuss both the Haggler case and Alana's mysterious disappearance.

The desk clerk greeted her with sobering news. "Your father hasn't checked in yet, Miss Drew," he informed her.

"Have there been any calls or messages?" Nancy asked.

The man checked, then shook his head.

Unhappy, Nancy accepted her key and went up to her attractive room. After about five minutes, she consulted the room service menu and ordered dinner. Waiting for her food only increased her unease and her feeling that something was wrong. Finally, she opened her address book and placed a call to Helen Haggler.

"Ah, Nancy, how are you?" Miss Haggler asked.

"A little anxious, Miss Haggler," Nancy admitted. "I've been missing connections with my father all day and I was wondering if you could tell me what time he left your home today."

"What time he what?" Miss Haggler sounded surprised. "I thought you were calling to set up another appointment."

"Another apointment?"

"Why, yes, I've been trying to reach him most of the day, myself." Miss Haggler sounded upset. "It's not like your father not to call, you know."

"But he was on his way to see you." Nancy said. "He left the hotel early this morning."

"Are you sure?"

"Of course. He wanted to talk to you about your change of mind. Are you saying he never reached your estate?" Nancy felt a cold stab of fear.

"I've been here all day," Helen Haggler replied. "He's neither arrived nor called. Haven't you heard from him?"

"No . . . well, sort of," Nancy amended. "I'm in Victoria." She explained how she'd come to be staying at the Creighton Hotel.

"Well, when you do see him, ask him to call, will you?" Miss Haggler said. "No matter how late it is."

"I'll do that," Nancy promised, but even as she spoke the words, she was afraid her father's disappearance was more than just a case of missed connections and changed plans.

8

A Cruel Bargain

When her food arrived, Nancy had little appe-
tite for it, but she ate, hoping the meal would
distract her from the fear inside her. She was
just finishing her dessert when the telephone
rang, so startlingly that she dropped her fork.

"Miss Nancy Drew?" The voice was male and
unfamiliar.

"This is she," Nancy replied.

"I'm calling about your father," the voice informed her.

"Where is he? Who is this? What's going on?"
The questions boiled out of her.

"Your father is with me," the voice answered
coldly.

"What do you mean he's with you?"

"All you need to know is that your father is

with me, and if you want to see him again, you're going to have to find Alana Steele for us."

"But I don't know where Alana is," Nancy protested. "I've been trying to find her."

"If you want your father back, don't make excuses." The voice was hard and ugly.

"How do I know you have my father?" Nancy asked, getting her fears under control with a stern effort of will.

"Listen to this," the voice ordered.

Nancy started to object, but there was a click and in a moment she heard her father's voice.

"Nancy, I'm all right. I'm being held . . . at a place and I'll be taken care of as long as you don't try to contact the authorities or anyone else. Don't try to find me. Just do as they tell you."

The tape clicked. "Dad!" Nancy moaned, aching to talk to him, to really hear his voice.

"If you want to talk to your father again, you'd better find Alana Steele," the voice told her unemotionally.'

"But I don't know where she is," Nancy wailed, desperation bringing tears to her eyes.

"You're a detective. You find her." There was a short bark of cruel laughter. "And remember what your father told you about contacting the authorities. If you do, you'll never see him again." The receiver clicked and the line went dead.

For a moment she sat still, tears flooding down her cheeks, her heart pounding with panic and fear. Then she remembered the sound of her father's voice, calm and strong, unafraid. She closed her eyes and tried to draw strength from his courage, his faith in her.

Alana was the key, she realized. But how? Who wanted to find Alana badly enough to actually kidnap Carson Drew? And why? There was only one reason that came to her mind—the missing sculpture, the Tundra.

Her mind once more working logically, Nancy picked up her purse and took out the notebook she'd found in Alana's room. It was now much easier for her to believe that someone had tried to harm Tod Harper, then gone to the mansion and slipped inside to search it.

"What could Alana know that makes her so important?" she asked herself, opening the notebook.

The first part of the notebook was simply a detailed cataloging of the individual carvings of the Tundra. Pages and pages listing caribou in various poses, the wolves, the bears, the tiny humans that populated the man-created tundra. Nancy skimmed through them, then noticed that several were starred.

"What's going on here?" she murmured, then she found the note at the end of the list.

"I've marked several carvings that seem very familiar to me," it read in Alana's handwriting. "If only I could remember where I've seen the ones like them."

The next section was devoted to research on the entire sculpture. There were notes about the owner, Franklin Cole, and his collection of Eskimo art, which included more than just the one piece. Only after she'd finished that did she find the more interesting part of the research that Alana had done and written down:

The Tundra has been a part of legend for quite some time. It is reputed to be the key to the mysterious disappearance of the ivory treasures of Seal Bay, a small Eskimo community once said to be the home of the most talented Eskimo carvers in the world.

These artists refused to sell any of their works, claiming they were a treasured part of their worship. The village fell on hard times, yet they still refused to sell and gradually all the collectors gave up—all but one. Franklin Cole continued to pressure the starving people.

At this time, according to legend, Qing-goq, the most talented artist of the village, gathered all their works and took them into the wilderness to hide them. The only piece left was his own masterpiece, the Tundra. This he refused to sell.

The hard times continued, mostly due to manipulations and tricks by Cole, and in the end the villagers decided to sell the Tundra to Cole in return for his promise never to enter Seal Bay again.

The legend ends with the story that the artist was enraged by the sale of his masterpiece to the man he considered the enemy of the village. He cursed the village and refused to return the treasures he'd hidden.

The story ended there and Nancy shook her head. It was fascinating, but she could see no relationship between an ancient legend and what was happening now. She flipped forward through the notebook, seeking more notes, something that would make this notebook valuable enough to risk capture by whoever had sought it at the Steele mansion.

There was nothing. The rest of the pages were blank.

"What did they want?" she asked herself,

looking around the anonymous hotel room in frustration. "What does this notebook have to do with the theft of the Tundra and how is Alana involved?"

The price of Carson Drew's freedom was finding Alana, and Nancy obviously wasn't going to be able to do it here. But where could she begin?

"Tod!" Nancy realized. She looked at her watch, feeling it must be nearly midnight, but it was just after seven P.M. Two quick phone calls located him at the nearby hospital. Not giving herself time to think ahead, Nancy hid the notebook in her suitcase, then picked up her purse and keys and hurried out of the hotel.

The hospital was fairly busy as visiting hours were ending, but Nancy had no trouble finding Tod's room. The door stood open, but she knocked anyway. His face was a mass of scrapes and bruises, but his grin seemed real enough.

"Nancy Drew, what are you doing here?" he asked.

"Well, since you missed our meeting this afternoon, I thought I'd come here and talk to you," Nancy began, feeling suddenly out of place and uncomfortable.

"You might be better off staying away from

me," Tod said, his grin fading. "Either that or stay off the streets. Don't you know what happened to me?"

"Who did this to you?" Nancy asked. And why, Tod?"

Tod began shifting in the bed, his eyes evading hers. "How would I know? It was an accident. Someone wasn't watching where he was going and I was cutting across the middle of the block. Just an accident."

"That's not what the officer told us," Nancy said.

"What officer? When?" Tod stopped his squirming. "What are you talking about?"

"There was a . . . someone got into the Steele mansion while I was downtown waiting for you. They searched Alana's room and mine. Do you have any idea what they were looking for?"

Their eyes locked for a moment and Nancy had the strong feeling Tod was trying to decide something.

"Probably Alana's notebook," Tod said at last, "if she didn't have it with her when she disappeared."

"Why would anyone want the notebook?" Nancy asked.

Tod shrugged. "I haven't the foggiest idea. Why would anyone steal an art object that would be impossible to sell legally or even show publicly?"

"Have you ever seen the notebook?" Nancy forced herself to sound casual, aware that she could frighten Tod off the subject.

"Only every day since we got the Tundra," Tod answered. "She cataloged it, then she started trying to research its history. The girl was really hooked on that piece."

"But do you know what was in the notebook?" Nancy asked.

"Not really. I mean she never told me or showed it to me. Why?"

"Then why do you think someone was after it?" Nancy had to ask.

Tod's face grew cold. "I think you should leave," he said.

"Talk to me, Tod," Nancy cried in desperation. "Help me find Alana. She called me asking for my help, but I can't do anything without help from you."

"Ask her uncle where she is," Tod growled. "I wasn't the inside man and I don't believe that Alana was, so that just leaves Clement Steele himself."

"So where is Alana?" Nancy asked.

Tod shook his head, then winced. "Go away, Nancy Drew," he said. "I can't help you."

"Can you tell me anything about what Alana was doing?" Nancy asked, controlling her panic and frustration with a firm hand. It was much easier to be a detective when she was just trying to solve a puzzle; knowing that her father's safety depended on her actions made it much harder. "Is there somewhere she might have gone? I think I remember her mentioning something called the Firebird."

Tod's eyes flickered to her face, but Nancy could read nothing more than surprise in them. "She wouldn't go there," he said.

"Why not?" It took all her control to keep her voice light, only mildly curious.

"That lodge is really run-down now. She must have been talking about the old days when it was a special place to stay. It's not even open to the public anymore as far as I know." He frowned. "What made you think of it?"

"The name I guess," Nancy answered casually. "It stuck in my mind. It sounds sort of special." She swallowed hard. "What about friends, Tod? Is there anyone who would hide her?"

"If you talked to her this afternoon, why didn't she tell you where she was?" Tod demanded, his eyes suddenly full of suspicion. "Why is it so important to you tonight?"

Nancy hesitated, longing to tell him the truth, longing to share her fears for her father with someone; but she couldn't trust him. As long as her father was in danger, she couldn't trust anyone. "Alana told me to forget her, to leave town before I became a victim," she answered honestly.

Tod's face grew grim. "She gave you good advice, Nancy Drew," he said. "Keep asking questions and you could end up like this . . . or worse!"

9

Dark Pursuit

Nancy caught her breath but before she could speak again, a nurse came to tell her she had to leave. She murmured a few words of polite farewell, then felt a chill as Tod simply looked at her. "Be careful," he warned, unsmiling. "They aren't playing games, Nancy."

Night had deepened to darkness while she was inside and in spite of the lights and people in the parking area, Nancy felt very much alone. She drove back to the hotel, stopping in the lobby only long enough to ask about the Firebird Lodge.

"It's located outside the city," the desk clerk said. "An old-fashioned place. Used to be quite well known, but it fell on hard times and I believe it's a kind of rooming house now. Were you planning on going out there?"

"I think someone there might be able to help my father and me with a case we're working on," Nancy said. "I just thought I'd get the address and perhaps a map of the area for my father."

"Is your father coming in tonight?" the desk clerk asked.

"Probably not till very late," Nancy said, wishing that the words were true, that she was expecting him to arrive. "I'll want you to hold the room, anyway, just so it will be ready for him."

The clerk nodded. "I'll get a map of the area and show you where the lodge is located," he said.

Nancy watched his drawing and listened attentively to what he said, but all the time she kept wondering if it was important. Tod hadn't seemed to think so, yet Alana had mentioned something about the secret of the Tundra being found at the Firebird. It was the only clue she had.

"I'll check it out in the morning," she told herself as she got into the elevator. At the moment she was so tired she wasn't sure she could make it down the long hall to her room. It had been an endless day.

And there was still the notebook, she reminded herself. Though she'd gone through it once, she realized that she hadn't known what she was looking for, so she might have missed something. Sighing, she unlocked the door and stepped inside, flipping on the light.

She gasped in horror at the sight that greeted her: the contents of her suitcase lay in a shambles. "I should have taken it with me," Nancy chided herself as she picked up the sweater within which she'd hid the notebook. The notebook was gone, of course.

Tears of frustration welled up. For a moment she was furious enough to call the authorities to report the break-in, but then she remembered the cold voice on the telephone and she knew she couldn't risk it.

"All right, you've won this round," she murmured to the empty room, "but I'm going to win the fight. I'm going to find Alana and learn this secret and then I'm going to get Dad and the Tundra back."

The words were brave, but they echoed in the empty room, underlining how alone she was. Nancy looked around and knew she couldn't stay.

Her eyes went to the map she still held. Could she find the place at night? She looked at the phone, then rejected the idea of calling ahead. "I hope you left me some clues, Alana," she said as she pulled on a jacket and prepared to leave the hotel again.

When she stepped out into the hall, however, she hesitated, suddenly realizing something. For anyone to have searched her room, they had to know she'd left the hotel. Were they watching her? She looked up and down the hall. It was empty and quiet. Someone in the lobby? That seemed more likely.

Nancy moved away from the elevators, following the hall to the far end where the stairs were located. She used them and smiled as she stepped out at the side of the hotel only a few yards from where her car was parked. "Now all I have to do is find Firebird Lodge," she told herself. "I just hope the desk clerk knew what he was drawing on this map."

The drive through Victoria was calming and gave her time to do a little thinking about all that had happened. The trouble was, her thoughts weren't very conclusive. Everyone seemed to have secrets. Alana, her uncle, Tod— they had all asked her to help; yet none of them had trusted her with the whole truth.

But what about her father? Nancy asked herself. Why kidnap him? She frowned at the night beyond her car windows. Obviously, he had been abducted before she went to Victoria; otherwise he would have arrived at the Haggler Estate.

Suddenly Nancy became aware of headlights behind her in the darkness. At first they were approaching quickly, then they seemed to slow until they were maintaining the same distance between their car and the rental one she was driving.

"Well, well, well, they must have been watching the car instead of the lobby," she murmured, wondering if they had followed her to the hospital, too. It would have been impossible to tell in the city traffic.

Nancy allowed the car to slow, trying to decide what to do. She couldn't just lead them to the lodge.

Should she return to the hotel? Her heart sank at the thought. She spread the map out next to her and studied it in the light from the dashboard. There were a number of roads in the area and some of them seemed to be connected. She had to lose the car that trailed her!

Nancy began watching for the road signs and when she spotted the one she was looking for, she sharply turned down the road, cut her lights, and drove as quickly as she could through the dark woods. For a moment there were no lights behind her and she felt a flash of joy. But then the lights appeared again.

Nancy turned her lights back on and pressed down hard on the accelerator. It was a mad race through the forest. The road twisted and turned, climbing and dropping, making the small car bounce over the rough spots. It became a nightmare of trees rearing out of the darkness and sudden squeals of tires as she veered around hidden curves.

Still the lights remained behind her, and it was obvious that her small rental car simply did not have the power to escape her pursuer.

The same thought seemed to occur to the driver of the chase car, and the lights loomed larger and larger as the driver closed the gap between them. Nancy looked around desperately, seeking a side road, anything; but the darkness was complete.

"You don't have me yet," she shouted as the big car pulled up alongside. She tried to accelerate, but her car simply couldn't go any faster. The bigger car loomed beside her and as she watched, the driver began to pull toward her, obviously trying to cut her off, to force her off the road and into the trees.

10

Secret at Firebird Lodge

Terrified, Nancy gripped the wheel until her knuckles gleamed white in the light from the dashboard. Then the driver of the other car jerked his wheel sharply. Nancy hit her brakes hard, letting her lighter car skid as the bigger, heavier car shot past her and sailed off the road to their right, past the trees and into a small open area.

Fighting the wheel, she managed to hold the car on the road as it lurched to a stop. Only then was she able to look to see what had happened to the other car.

The silence of the night was broken by motor sounds and as Nancy slowly turned her small car around, her lights shone on the bigger one. Relieved, Nancy began to laugh nervously.

The clearing was a boggy area, and the car had sunk to its fenders as the driver raced the motor and spun the buried tires.

Still shaking from the ordeal, Nancy drove slowly back the way she'd come. Whenever she saw a sign, she stopped to read it, checking her map until she came upon a sign overgrown with vines that said it was two miles to Firebird Lodge. She turned onto the rutted road.

"The way things have been going, the place will probably be closed," she told herself grimly.

The road wasn't promising. Weeds grew in the middle and the trees were so thick and tall they met overhead, creating a dark, menacing tunnel. Still, she eventually reached the end of the road and a hulking building with lights on waiting to greet her.

Not sure what she was going to say, Nancy parked in a row of three cars and turned off the motor. For the first time since she'd discovered she was being followed she relaxed. She leaned against the seat and smoothed back her hair from her damp forehead as the door of the lodge opened.

To Nancy's amazement, Alana Steele stood in the path of the light. Feeling as if she were in a dream, Nancy opened the car door and stepped out, then leaned weakly on the fender.

"Nancy, Nancy, is that you?" Alana called. "How did you find us?"

"Us?" Nancy was suddenly aware of the young man standing behind her friend, and she felt a chill of apprehension. He must have been the one who placed Alana's call to the Steele mansion.

"Are you all right, Nancy?" Alana gasped, hurrying forward.

"I think so," Nancy replied. "There was a car chasing me. They tried to force me off the road, but they ended up in a bog."

"Come inside, please," the man said. "You can ask each other questions there. I think your friend could use some hot tea or maybe cocoa, Alana."

Nancy nodded, allowing Alana to take her arm and lead her up the steps and into the large front room of the old log building. She said nothing until she was seated on an old, worn couch and holding a warm mug in her still-cold hands.

"How did you find me?" Alana asked.

"You mentioned the Firebird," Nancy explained. "The last time you called, you said you'd found the secret of the Tundra here. I didn't know where else to start."

"I called to tell you to go back to Seattle," Alana reminded her.

"I can't," Nancy said simply. She looked up

at the man who'd returned from the rear of the lodge with a plate of brownies. He was a young man of Eskimo descent and his dark eyes and smile seemed quite friendly.

"This is Ben Qinggoq," Alana said. "His grandfather was the master artist who created the Tundra."

Nancy shook hands with the young man, but her frown stayed in place. "I don't understand," she admitted. "What's the discovery you made at Firebird Lodge?"

"When I was cataloging the individual carvings in the Tundra, I kept feeling I'd seen some of them before," Alana began. "It haunted me. Then the day you called me, I remembered where I'd seen such carvings. They were here." She pointed to the mantel.

"Here?" Nancy got to her feet and crossed to the huge, smoke-darkened slab of wood that stood above the inlaid stone fireplace. As soon as she drew close, she could see what Alana meant. There was a whole series of creatures carved in the edge of the mantel.

"My parents brought me here when I was just a child. They were visiting Uncle Clement, but all I remembered were those carvings. I loved them so much."

"They're exquisite," Nancy murmured tracing one with the tip of her finger. "But I still don't understand why it was so important."

"When the Firebird Lodge was being used for tourists, the mantel was quite a celebrated piece," Ben Qinggoq said, coming to stand beside Nancy. "My grandfather was an angry, stubborn man. He'd refused to show any more work after the villagers sold the Tundra, but his name and his talent were still known to collectors and this was the only example of it still available. People came here to see the mantel and to talk about the legend of the Tundra."

Alana nodded. "The owners of the lodge even had a brochure printed up showing the mantel and telling the legend about the man who'd carved it. I had the brochure, and when I came upon it recently, I had the whole story. That's when I knew why the Tundra was stolen and by whom."

Nancy stared at the quiet brunette in shock. "You know who stole the Tundra?" she gasped.

Alana's gray eyes warmed and she smiled. "As soon as I knew why it was taken, it was easy to figure out who took it," she explained.

"But why didn't you call someone?" Nancy demanded. "The authorities suspect you or your uncle of stealing it, Alana. And your uncle is frantic with worry about you." Then Nancy suddenly remembered the tape recording of her father's voice and the warning she'd been given.

"It's not quite that simple, Nancy," Alana said.

"What do you mean?"

"I've been hiding here ever since I escaped," Alana answered. "And I can't go home because I can't go to the authorities."

Nancy made a sputtering noise of frustration as all the questions tripped over her tongue. "Escaped from whom?" she finally managed.

"From Jasper Cole and Felix Borge," Alana answered.

"Cole?" Nancy frowned.

"A nephew of the original purchaser of the Tundra," Ben supplied.

Alana nodded. "They were also former partners of Franklin Cole," she explained. "Junior partners, I'd guess, since they're men in their late thirties, and Franklin Cole was in his seventies when he died. Anyway, they told me they'd worked with him on his collection when they approached me with offers of information about the history of the Tundra."

"They approached *you?*" Nancy began to see the first outlines of the pattern of what Alana was telling her.

"At the time, I just thought they were being helpful," Alana admitted ruefully. "They did give me some information. I just didn't realize they were getting as much information from me as they were supplying."

"What kind of information?" Nancy asked.

Alana's expression grew sad. "It doesn't matter. I finally realized what was happening and that's when I talked to you the first time. At that moment, I thought you might be able to help; but it was already too late."

"Too late for what?" Nancy frowned, not liking the turn of the conversation.

"An hour later I was kidnapped," Alana answered simply.

11

Searching a Legend

"Kidnapped?" Nancy felt a chill at the similarity between Alana's story and what had happened to her father.

"Lured from the house by a phone call, then I was knocked out. Anyway, one minute I was sitting in my car waiting to talk to someone about the Tundra, and the next minute I woke up in the hold of an old boat. I never saw anyone or heard anything. There were no portholes in the boat and the door was barred. There was food and water. I don't even know how long I was locked in."

"How terrible." Nancy shivered. "How did you escape?"

"That's where Ben comes in," Alana said.

The Eskimo smiled shyly. "I fish at dawn

most days," he said. "I'd noticed the old boat anchored near the island and I was curious. The fish weren't biting, so I went closer for a look. I heard someone beating on the hull and screaming for help. It was Alana."

"And you rescued her." It wasn't a question. Hope flooded through Nancy. If one kidnap victim had been placed in a boat, why not a second? "Where is this boat?" Nancy asked. "Whom does it belong to?"

Ben looked startled. "I don't know."

"You don't know where it is?"

He shook his head. "I went back to check it once Alana was safely hidden here with my friends, but it was gone."

"They must have gone out to get me," Alana said, smiling. "I'll bet they were surprised to find the cabin empty."

"Who are they?" Nancy asked.

"Cole and Borge," Alana answered without hesitation.

"If you know, why haven't you gone to the authorities?" Nancy demanded.

"I can't do that to Uncle Clement," Alana answered.

"What does he have to do with it?" Nancy asked.

"When I got here, the TV and the papers were full of details of the robbery," Alana said.

"That's when I knew what the kidnappers had demanded as the ransom for me—the Tundra." Her smile was sad. "Uncle Clement gave it to them in exchange for my life."

"Well, if that's true, why can't you go to the authorities? Once they know the whole story, your uncle won't be blamed."

"Without proof?" Alana asked. "Do you think they would believe me?"

"Well, Ben would tell them about finding you," Nancy reminded her.

Alana considered, then shook her head. "I don't think they would believe us," she said. "And even if they do, do you think any collector would ever trust the Steele Gallery again? My uncle would be ruined and it would be all my fault."

"It wasn't your fault you were kidnapped," Nancy protested. "Besides, none of this makes any sense, Alana. If those men were Franklin Cole's partners, why didn't they just buy the Tundra from his widow? Why would they steal it?"

"That's the piece of the puzzle that Ben gave me," Alana said. "Will you explain it to her?"

Ben sighed. "The Tundra, beautiful as it is, has a value beyond itself. The legend is true. The secret that gives the location of the treasures my grandfather took from Seal Bay is concealed within that sculpture. That's why those two were so anxious to have it."

"But how did they know?" Nancy asked.

"Franklin Cole probably," Ben answered. "I imagine he knew the story well, since he was a part of it in the beginning. That's why he never would show the Tundra. I guess he always believed he'd figure it out someday."

"But he didn't, did he?" Nancy said.

"No, and so his partners are trying to complete Franklin Cole's dream," Ben agreed.

Nancy nodded. "But where do you fit in, Ben?" she asked.

"I came to Victoria for the same reason," Ben replied. "Only I was just going to look at the Tundra while it was on display."

"Do you know the secret of the sculpture?" Nancy gasped.

"According to the old men of Seal Bay, I do," he answered. "They gave me a message from my grandfather, words he told them when he knew he was dying. You see, he'd never told anyone where the treasures were hidden. That was his punishment to them for having sold his treasures—that and the fact that he told them the Tundra was the key. Unfortunately, what he told them makes no sense at all to me. I came here hoping that if I studied the Tundra carefully, I

94

could figure out what his words mean."

"And now it's gone and Ben won't have the chance," Alana said. "Again, it's all my fault, Nancy."

"Do you think Cole and Borge can find the treasure now that they have the Tundra?" Nancy asked.

Alana shrugged, then looked to Ben for the answer.

He shook his head. "I doubt it. Franklin Cole had years to study it. Without the secret my grandfather knew, it is just a beautiful masterpiece—a priceless collection of his carvings."

"I guess that explains something else," Nancy said.

"What do you mean?" Alana said.

Nancy took a deep breath and explained about her father's disappearance and the call she'd received at the hotel.

"You mean they want me?" Alana gasped.

Nancy nodded. "They seem to think you know the secret of the sculpture."

Alana closed her eyes as though in pain. "They're wrong, of course."

"But they have my father."

"Even I couldn't help them solve it," Ben said.

"What are we going to do?" Alana asked. "I

don't know anyone to ask for help. I tried to call Tod to ask him to tell my uncle I'm all right, but there was no answer at his apartment."

"Tod is in the hospital," Nancy interrupted. "Besides, I think his phone may be tapped." She quickly explained about Tod's accident and the break-in that had occurred that afternoon. Alana was even more upset by this news.

"I know how they got into the house," Alana said sadly. "They took my keys when they kidnapped me." She sighed. "But why would they do that? Why search the house?"

"They were evidently looking for your notebook." Nancy explained how she had found it in Alana's room.

"But it wouldn't have helped them to solve anything," Alana protested.

"I'm sure they know that now," Nancy told her. "They didn't get it the first time because I had it in my purse, but they did get it the second time. I left it in the room when I went to visit Tod."

"These people are so desperate now," Ben said. "I wonder why they didn't just buy the piece from the widow. Surely she would have let them have it since they were her husband's former partners."

Alana shook her head. "I don't think so. She

was very adamant about the sale of the Tundra. She told Uncle Clement that it wasn't to be sold to anyone who wouldn't display it. I got the feeling that it was something she and her husband had quarreled about for years."

"I'm surprised they didn't have someone else make an offer for them," Nancy said. "A slightly fraudulent purchase would certainly have been less risky than an out-and-out theft, even with your uncle forced into helping them."

"They probably did," Alana said. "Mrs. Cole warned Uncle Clement to check out every prospective buyer very carefully."

Nancy sighed wearily. "We have to stop them," she said. "And we have to get Dad back."

"But how?" Alana asked.

The sound of a car door loudly slamming out in front of the lodge interrupted her.

"Could that be the men who were chasing you earlier?" Ben remarked, his gaze going to Nancy.

She could only shrug as he flipped off the overhead lamp and moved on tiptoe to the window. The light from the flickering fireplace made eerie shadows and they could all hear the sounds of footsteps on the creaking boards of the wide front porch.

12

Uncertain Flight

Nancy got to her feet and joined Ben at the window. The car was parked in a patch of moonlight bright enough to show the marks of mud that had dried nearly halfway up the sides.

"It's those men," she whispered.

"What'll we do?" Alana gasped.

"You two go out the back door and circle around to the front," Ben ordered. "They don't know me, so I'll talk to them."

"We'll stay near my car," Nancy said, "in case we have to leave in a hurry."

The girls nodded, and Nancy followed Alana toward the rear of the old lodge. Once they left the lobby, the darkness was so complete she could see nothing but the pale blur of her friend's blouse. The halls were uncluttered and

Alana moved with confidence until they reached the dimly lit kitchen. Here Alana paused for a moment.

Nancy slipped by her and peered out the kitchen window. The area beyond was dark, and tall evergreens shadowed the house. There was no sign of movement there. "I think it's safe," she whispered, even as the pounding sounds came from the front of the house.

Alana opened the door and the two of them stepped out into the cool darkness. The sound of the pounding was still audible. A man's voice shouted for admittance. Then abruptly the sounds ceased. Nancy followed around the crossed-log corners of the house toward the front.

"What do you want?" Ben asked, somehow managing to sound both angry and sleepy.

"We're here to see Nancy Drew," one of the men said.

"There's no one here by that name," Ben told them calmly.

"Her car is out in your lot," the man grumbled, not giving up.

"I can't help that. She's not here." Ben didn't yield an inch.

"I don't believe you."

"I don't really care whether you do or not.

Now if you'll just get on your way, I'd appreciate it. All this noise will disturb the people who live here. We—" Ben's words were interrupted by the sounds of a scuffle, then the door slammed. Nancy peeked in the living room window and saw two men standing in the lobby with Ben.

"Are those two Cole and Borge?" Nancy whispered to Alana.

Alana peeked in, and then shook her head. "I've never seen them before, but that voice is familiar. I heard it once when I met with Cole and Borge to discuss the history of the Tundra. I'm sure he works for them, so they probably both do."

"Out of our way," the bigger man snarled, shoving Ben to one side. "We're going to find the girl."

Ben started to swing, then seemed to think better of it. "Search if you like," he said. "Just try not to disturb any of the people upstairs. They might call the police about burglars like you."

The other man chuckled evilly. "Not on your phone lines," he said.

Alana and Nancy gasped and looked around. It took only a moment to spot the cut lines.

"What are we going to do, Nancy?" Alana whispered.

"We're going to get out of here," Nancy replied. "Come on."

They left the protection of the log structure and made their way through the trees to where the cars were parked. Nancy studied them, then grinned. "Let's let the air out of two tires on every car," she said. "Except for mine, of course."

Alana started to protest, then she giggled. "Even my car?" she asked.

Nancy considered for a moment, aware that Alana's car was bigger and more powerful, then she nodded. "The authorities must be looking for your car," she said. "We'll be much safer in my rental."

"Okay, Nancy," Alana agreed.

There were some angry shouts from inside the lodge. Nancy looked up as lights went on behind some of the windows. "I hope they don't hurt anyone," she murmured, feeling guilty for having led the men to this refuge.

"Don't worry about the people who live at the Firebird," Alana said. "They're well able to take care of themselves. Those two may find themselves tossed out, if they get too pushy."

The girls moved from car to car leaving a trail of flat tires behind them. They'd just finished the last car when a dark form detached itself from the shadows. "What are you two doing?" Ben asked.

"Just slowing down the enemy," Nancy said.

"How about letting me put the finishing touches on their car," Ben said, releasing the hood of the big, mud-caked sedan. "You get your car started, Nancy. We don't want to be here when they come out."

Nancy did as he suggested, feeling better than she had since the phone call about her father. She was really no closer to rescuing him, but at least she had gained some information as well as Alana's and Ben's help.

"Let's go," Ben said, getting into the back-seat.

Nancy swung the small car around and headed down the rutted road just as the door of the lodge opened and the two men came racing out. Their shouts range in her ears.

"What about your friends at the lodge?' Nancy asked. "How will they manage with their cars disabled and the phone lines out?"

"When they get ready to leave, they'll just hike down to the harbor and take their fishing boats out," Ben said. "Your playmates are the

102

only ones who are going to be stuck at the lodge for a while."

"What a shame," Nancy said, laughing.

Alana sighed. "So what do we do now?" she asked.

Nancy's high spirits dropped. "I really don't know," she admitted.

"I still can't go to the authorities," Alana said.

"I couldn't let you, anyway, not while they have my dad," Nancy reminded her.

"We need to come up with a plan," Ben said. "A way to get your father back, Nancy, and to trick those crooks into giving up the Tundra. If we could do that, we could clear up everything."

Nancy nodded. "Sounds like the perfect solution. Do you have a plan?"

"Not a hint of one," he admitted.

"How about you, Nancy?" Alana asked.

Nancy bit her lip. "I don't have any ideas either," she said. "I just know we have to be very careful. I don't want Dad to get hurt."

"Don't even think about that," Alana said. "They're not going to do anything to him, not when they think they can trade him for me."

"I wouldn't do that, Alana," Nancy told her. "You know I wouldn't. No matter what they say."

"I think we have a more immediate problem," Ben interrupted.

"What's that?" Nancy asked.

"Where to go now. Those two are going to be stuck at the Firebird for a while, but once they get away, they'll look for us again and I don't know of any other place to hide Alana."

"I wish we could go to my uncle," Alan said, "but I'm sure he's being watched and I can't bring him any more trouble."

"Well, you know, the kidnappers were kind enough to reserve two rooms at the hotel for my father and me, so I suggest we use them," Nancy said. "What do you think?"

"You mean stay at your hotel?" Alana and Ben chorused.

"Well, they've been watching it pretty closely but since they obviously followed me when I left earlier, there's probably no one watching now."

"That's crazy," Alana protested.

"Why?" Nancy asked. "I *have* to be there so they can contact me about Dad."

"You're right," Alana admitted. "I'm sorry, Nancy. I guess I've been thinking of my own problems so long that I'd forgotten other people have trouble, too."

"Anyway, think about it, you two. I can go in

first and pick up Dad's key, then I'll go to the fire door and let you in so no one will see you." Nancy grinned at them. "Don't you think the hotel will be the last place that anyone would look for you, Alana?"

Ben and Alana exchanged glances, then shrugged. "I guess we really don't have much choice," Alana said. "I just don't want to put you in any more danger, Nancy. What's happened to you and your father is all my fault."

"I called you, Alana," Nancy reminded her.

"But I asked you to help me," Alana said.

"And warned me to leave before I got too involved. Besides, I have a feeling that we still don't have the whole story."

"But what else could there be?" Ben asked.

"My father was kidnapped before I came to Victoria," Nancy said. "I mean he must have been, because he left the hotel in Seattle hours before I did and he never reached the Haggler estate."

"The Haggler estate?" Alana said. "You mean the Haggler that has all those terrific import shops?"

"You've heard of them?" Nancy was a little surprised.

"You can't be interested in art and not know about Haggler International Imports," Alana declared. "Miss Haggler has imported some really fabulous things and she does occasionally handle Northern Indian or Eskimo art, too, you know. Everything in her shops doesn't come from Japan or China or Europe or South America."

"Sounds like you've checked them out pretty carefully," Ben teased.

"When your uncle runs a gallery and eats, sleeps, and breathes art, you get to see a lot of import shops," Alana replied with a small giggle. "Was your father working for Miss Haggler?"

Nancy nodded. 'That's why we were in Seattle."

"I just wish you hadn't been," Alana said, her good spirits fading as quickly as they'd come. "I wanted to see you, but not like this."

"This will be cleared up soon," Nancy told her as she turned in to the hotel parking lot. "And after it is, we'll have a real visit."

"I'll even take you and your father out fishing, if you like," Ben said.

Nancy gave him a grateful smile, aware that he, too, was trying to remain optimistic. "Now," she said. "You two say in the car for a while, then just casually make your way around to the far side there. The fire door opens just past that flowerbed. I'll get there as soon as I can."

"We'll be there," Ben promised. "You be careful."

Nancy nodded. "After all that's happened, I will be," she said.

The hotel lobby was nearly empty when she entered, reminding her for the first time of the lateness of the hour. Though she still had her own room key, she headed directly for the desk. There was a different clerk on duty, so she simply asked about a reservation for Carson Drew, signing her father's name to the register.

"Oh, Miss Drew, you have some messages," the clerk said when he handed her the key.

"Messages?" Nancy swallowed hard.

"There have been a number of calls." The clerk handed her the list.

"Thank you," Nancy said. There was only one name on the list, but the messages had become increasingly urgent. Helen Haggler was desperately trying to reach Carson Drew and she wanted him to call—no matter what time it was. If she did not hear from him by morning, she would contact the police!

13

Stalling for Time

Nancy started toward the elevators, then hesitated, suddenly remembering what had happened to Tod after her telephone conversation with him. The men had been in her hotel room; the missing notebook was proof of that. She had no way of knowing if they'd bugged the telephone while she was away.

Nancy headed for the public telephones, closing herself in a booth and placing a call to Miss Haggler.

"Carson?" Helen Haggler began as soon as she'd accepted the collect call.

"No, Miss Haggler, it's Nancy," the girl said.

"Where's your father?" Miss Haggler asked. "Has he arrived there?"

"He's in Victoria," Nancy began, "but he isn't at the hotel."

"Have you talked to him?"

"I've heard from him," Nancy replied, choosing her words carefully, trying to avoid an outright lie, yet also wanting to keep the real situation from the woman.

"Nancy, give me a straight answer," Helena snapped. "Have you seen your father?"

"No." Nancy couldn't keep her tone from showing her desperation.

"Has he been kidnapped?"

"Kidnapped?" Nancy swallowed hard. "What makes you think that, Miss Haggler?"

"So something *has* happened to him." The woman sounded as weary and discouraged as Nancy felt.

"They warned me," Miss Haggler said. "They said to drop the investigation or accept the consequences. I expected maybe another warehouse fire or an interruption in a shipment from a foreign port. I never dreamed they would strike so close to home."

"Who?" Nancy demanded, recovering her senses. "What are you talking about?"

"I'm talking about the men behind Investors, Inc., of course. Why do you think I told your

109

father that I wanted to call off the investigation. I was trying to buy some time, time to build up my security at all the shops, time to warn all my import people, my foreign buyers. I just wanted time to set up some sort of trap."

"Is that what you and Dad were going to discuss?" Nancy asked. "Had you told him?"

"I was going to tell him when he got here," Helen Haggler answered. "I don't ordinarily discuss things like that over the telephone."

"Did anyone else know what you were planning?" Nancy asked, her frown deepening.

"Just my board of directors. I had to tell them about the new threat, but surely none of them would betray me." Her tone had changed to one of speculation.

Nancy hesitated for a moment, her mind whirling. She didn't know what to say.

"Where is your father?" Miss Haggler asked again.

"He's being held somewhere," Nancy replied, making her decision. "He's safe as long as I don't call in the authorities and do what his kidnappers want."

"What do they want?" Helen asked. "Is it my corporation?"

"No, no, it has nothing to do with you," Nancy answered. "It's another matter entirely, some-

110

thing that I was working on here in Victoria. I'm making ransom arrangements now, so please, Miss Haggler, for Dad's sake, don't do anything to jeopardize them. Just wait and he'll be calling you himself."

"You can't deal with that sort of person," Miss Haggler warned. "You can't trust them, Nancy. You need help."

"I have it," Nancy replied, stretching the truth a little. "I have friends with me now, some of the people involved in the case, so it will be all right. Please trust me."

There was a long moment of silence and Nancy held her breath, well aware that her father's safety could depend on Helen Haggler's cooperation. Finally the woman sighed. "I'll give you until this time tomorrow night," she said. "If I don't hear from Carson by then, I'm going to report his disappearance and stir up a manhunt that will put all these crooks out of business for good."

"Midnight tomorrow night," Nancy murmured, closing her eyes for a moment to offer a silent prayer that it would be long enough. "I'll be in touch before then."

"Not you, Nancy," Miss Haggler corrected. "I want to talk to Carson before that. Understand? I don't care what other cases he's working on.

111

He was on his way to talk to me and I feel responsible for his disappearance."

"He'll call you," Nancy promised, hoping she was telling the truth.

"You take care of yourself, too," Miss Haggler continued. "I know how much confidence your father has in your abilities, but this must be a dreadful time for you. If there is anything I can do, just let me know—day or night."

"Thank you," Nancy replied, "and thank you for caring."

"Just get Carson back."

"I'll do my best." Nancy replaced the receiver, feeling drained. She leaned against the cool metal for a moment, then she remembered that Alana and Ben would be waiting for her. In spite of her exhaustion, the night was not yet over.

She took the elevator to her floor, then hurried along the hall to the stairs. Once there she took a bandage from her purse and used it to keep the door to the stairway from locking. The doors to the stairs, which were meant only as a fire exit, had no knobs on the inside, so they couldn't be opened except from the hall or with a key. Once she was sure she could get back into the hall, she hurried down to the first floor and cautiously opened the exit door.

"Where have you been?" Alana demanded. "We've been waiting forever."

"I'm sorry, but I had to take care of something," Nancy said, then explained about Miss Haggler's call, finishing, "I couldn't risk her calling the police in Seattle and I was afraid the phone in my room might have been bugged."

Alana nodded. "We have to keep anyone else from knowing what is going on."

"Anyway, let's get back upstairs and out of sight," Nancy said.

"This really is very kind of you," Ben commented.

"You're a part of this, too," Nancy reminded him. "After all, the Tundra is your heritage."

"And the treasures could give my people a real chance," Ben agreed. "If they had those carvings back, they could sell some and build the school and the other things they need in Seal Bay. The settlement never really recovered from what Cole did to it when he was trying to force the artists to sell him their works."

"What do you mean?" Nancy asked, stopping for a moment to catch her breath on the long climb.

"There's nothing there for the young people. I left as soon as I could and so do many of the

113

others. It's a town without a future, unless something is done. I think my grandfather was beginning to realize that and to feel guilty toward the end. I just wish he'd entrusted the secret to someone else—someone who could solve the riddle of the Tundra."

"We'll solve it," Nancy assured him with more confidence than she truly felt. "Just as soon as we get it back."

"That's what I like," Alana said. "Confidence!"

They waited while Nancy peeled the tape off the door, then followed her down the hall to her room. Nancy handed Ben the key she'd just gotten from the desk clerk. "Your room is right there," she said, indicating the door next to hers, "but why don't you come in with us first. Maybe we can come up with a plan."

"I hope you have some ideas," Alana said as Nancy unlocked the door. "I, for one, have just about run out. She stopped as Nancy grabbed her arm. "What is it?"

"I'm sure I turned off the lights when I left," Nancy said, looking around. Then she saw it— a small tape player resting on the dresser, waiting for them.

14

A Puzzling Code

"Let me check," Ben said, moving past the two girls to look in the bath and closet. "There's no one here," he told them. "Maybe you just forgot about the lights."

Nancy shook her head. "They've been here," she said. "They just made a delivery."

"What do you mean?" Alana asked.

Nancy crossed to the dresser and looked down at the tape player. "They brought this," she replied.

"A message?" Ben asked.

"Or instructions," Nancy suggested.

"For what?" Alana looked pale. "Do you think they know you've found me?"

Nancy shrugged. "Your car was at the lodge," she reminded her. "I'm sure they saw it after we left, even if they didn't notice it before."

"What are we going to do?" Ben inquired.

"I guess the only way we'll know for sure what's going on is to play this," Nancy said. "We might as well sit down and relax."

They settled themselves about the room, but no one was relaxed. Nancy pressed the button with a real feeling of fear—for her father and for her friends.

"Nancy." The voice was her father's and she felt a quick swelling of relief just hearing it. "I've explained to these . . . gentlemen that they must allow you to make some business calls for me. The various cases I was handling in Seattle all included appointments I either missed today or will miss tomorrow.

"These matters are crucial to the clients and if they cannot reach me by telephone for an explanation, several of them will be angry enough to call the police and institute a manhunt. My kidnappers have no desire for the spotlight at this time. I will give you a list of clients, phone numbers, and messages to be delivered."

"Clients?" Nancy whispered. "We were working on one case, and I've already talked to her."

"It is imperative, Nancy, that you spread oil on the waters with these people and convince them that I am working on their cases. Just be sure you don't tell one about the others. Let each one think I'm working exclusively for him or her."

The tone and voice were smooth and businesslike, the instructions given as concisely as though her father were sitting at the desk before her. All that was wrong was that the instructions concentrated on clients and cases that didn't exist.

The list of names, numbers, and messages went on for several minutes, then her father sighed, "That's it, Nancy, if you can handle the ACB's of my clients, we can progress with what has to be done to win my freedom." The tape ended.

"What's wrong, Nancy?" Alana asked.

Nancy shook her head and laughed, rewinding the tape. "Nothing is wrong," she said. "In fact something is very right, if I can just make sense of this."

"What is there to make sense of?" Ben asked. "It sounded pretty routine to me."

"Oh, it is," Nancy agreed. "Except that most of these clients and cases exist only in my father's mind or in our history. We were in Seattle working on the Haggler case, period."

Alana frowned, then her expression cleared and she laughed. "It's a code, right?"

"It's a message," Nancy said, "but not in any kind of code that's easy to decipher. He obviously had no time to work out any precise system. I'm going to have to take all this down and try to reason out his message with each name, number, and message."

Ben whistled. "That sounds very difficult."

"It's our best chance yet," Nancy said. "If I can figure our what he means, I'll bet it will tell us where he is, who is holding him, and how we can rescue him." She got a small notebook and pen from her purse and started the tape again. "I have to take this down word for word."

The telephone stopped her. Nancy shut off the tape player and, after a nervous look at Ben and Alana, picked up the receiver. Her hello sounded a great deal more confident than she felt.

"Nancy Drew?"

"Speaking."

"It's about time you got back." It was the same voice as the first call.

"You told me to find Alana," Nancy replied coldly. "I can't do that sitting around a hotel room."

"Did you find her?" The voice frightened her.

"Not yet," Nancy said. "I did manage to find

118

out where she's been hiding, but I arrived too late. She'd already made arrangements for a different car and some kind of disguise." She had to bite her lip to keep from giggling at the expressions on Ben's and Alana's faces as they listened to her.

"There was someone else in the car with you when you left," the voice said, making it clear the men had managed to escape from the Firebird Lodge.

"The man who helped her," Nancy admitted. "He's an old friend of Alana's, and your men scared him pretty badly. I'm going to have to try to convince him to trust me, but it won't be easy with your thugs following me around."

Ben looked insulted, then amused by her words.

"Are you threatening me, Nancy Drew?" the voice asked.

"I'm just telling you that I can't do what you want me to if you keep blocking me. You have my father and you know I'll do anything to get him back safely. But I can't locate Alana if you frighten her away before I can reach her."

There was a long silence from the other end. Nancy covered the mouthpiece and took a couple of deep breaths to steady herself. She could be in desperate trouble if they knew she wasn't telling the truth. If they believed her, she could buy time. That was what she needed most, she realized. Time to think and to study what her father had tried to tell her on the tape. Everything had happened too fast so far; she'd had to rely on intuition and quick responses. Now she needed a plan.

"You do believe you can find her?"

"I have to," Nancy answered quietly. "For my father's sake."

"I'm glad you've decided to be cooperative," the voice said, warming slightly. "Did you find the tape?"

"Of course. I was just listening to it."

"You will carry out your father's instructions?"

"To keep him safe, naturally. However, I can't do anything until tomorrow morning."

"Why not?" The suspicion was back.

"Because lawyers don't call clients in the middle of the night unless it's an emergency and I don't think you want to make our clients suspicious about my father's disappearance."

Again there was a moment of silence, then a sigh. "I suppose that's correct, as long as they don't report him missing before you call."

"I'll make sure that they don't," Nancy assured him.

"What about Alana Steele?"

"That will have to wait until tomorrow, too," Nancy said. "When I talk to her friend again, I'll try to find out where she might be hiding. But that could take a little time."

"You don't have much," the voice snarled, "We can't wait for long."

"But I'm doing my best." Nancy allowed her real feelings of desperation to show in her voice. "Please don't hurt my father. I'll find Alana somehow. Just don't hurt him!"

"We'll be in touch." The phone clicked dead. Nancy replaced her own receiver and closed her eyes for a moment.

"You were wonderful, Nancy," Alana said.

"Did they believe you?" Ben asked.

"I think so," Nancy said. "If they had known that Alana was with me, they would have come after her."

"So what's our next move?" Alana asked, yawning.

"Sleep, I think," Nancy said. "I'll write down everything from the tape, then sleep on it. Right now I don't think I could decipher anything."

Ben nodded, getting to his feet. "Pound on the wall if you need me," he said, then grinned, his black eyes dancing. "I'm really not afraid of those crooks."

"Sorry," Nancy apologized with a giggle. "I

thought it was better if they didn't see you as a threat."

"I know," he assured her. "I just hope I get a chance to show them how I really feel."

"I hope we all do," Nancy said.

Nancy worked on transcribing from the tape while Alana got ready for bed. A final check made her sure she had everything down exactly as he'd said it, but the words swam before her aching eyes and refused to make any sense to her.

"You look worse than I feel," Alana told her.

"I just hate to give up," Nancy admitted. "Every minute can be important to Dad. I have to figure out what he was trying to tell me."

"Nancy, there is something." Alana's serious tone brought Nancy's attention away from the words.

"What is it?" she asked.

"If it comes right down to it. If we can't figure out a way to trick them, I want you to make the exchange. I'll go to them. I can't help them, but if they'll set your father free, it's worth it. It's my fault that all of you are involved in this mess. If I hadn't asked so many questions about the Tundra, maybe none of this would have happened."

Nancy went over to hug her friend. "Thanks, Alana," she said, "but I couldn't do that."

"I'm not asking you to, I'm just telling you what *I'll* do," Alana stated firmly.

"But it wouldn't work," Nancy told her gently. "Don't you see, they can't let my father go. He knows far too much about them already.

Alana's face grew pale and her grey eyes widened in horror.

"We're his only hope," Nancy said.

15

Message in Pieces

In spite of the late hour when she went to bed, Nancy woke shortly after dawn. Alana was still sleeping soundly, so Nancy moved to the small table in front of the window and began to study the words she'd written down.

Some of it made perfect sense, but there were so many phrases that just didn't sound like her father. She began underlining the things that sounded wrong.

Spotlight at this time. Oil on the waters. The whole portion about not telling one about the others. All the names, numbers, and messages except for Helen Haggler and, in his final words, his saying *ACB's.*

These were not accidental words, she was sure of it, even though they were delivered without the slightest emphasis. Glaring at them, she knew she'd chosen the right phrases as clues, but she lacked the key that would make sense of them. She turned her attention to the names.

Ned Nickerson. Nancy smiled. Obviously not a client since he and Nancy were dating. *Okay the Merritt case* was the message.

"Merritt, Merritt," Nancy murmured, then grinned. "Merritt Island," she crowed, then put her hand over her mouth quickly, looking toward Alana. Her friend stirred, moaned, and was quiet again. Merritt Island was in Florida and Ned's parents owned a home there, one that Nancy had visited.

Mr. DeFoe. Another familiar name, this time from a past case. *The missing horse Polka Dot has been located and I have put in a claim.* Nancy shook her head. The *Polka Dot* was a boat, not a horse.

"Boat. Island. Oil on water." Nancy began to laugh softly. It had to be her father's way of telling her that he was being held on an island. But what island. Her smile faded. *Spotlight.* A lighthouse? That made sense.

The next name referred to another case in which her father had to distribute an inheritance among three claimants. Three men. The number of men on the island with him?

The fourth name was *Helen Haggler* and the number was correct. The message, however, surprised her a little. *Instincts correct. Case closed.* A warning to Miss Haggler? Nancy decided that's what it meant and to call Miss Haggler and relay it. With luck, it should buy them a little more time.

The fifth name referred to an art fraud case in which the masterpiece had been saved at the last minute by their surprise invasion of the old mansion where it was hidden. That could be interpreted to mean that the Tundra was being held at the same location he was.

Nancy leaned back in her chair, feeling much better. Only one more name to go and she had a whole selection of clues to work on. No answers yet, of course, but at least her father had given her some signposts to follow.

"What are you grinning about?' Alana asked, snapping Nancy back to the present. "Have you solved the mystery tape?"

"Not all of it," Nancy answered. "But it is beginning to make sense to me."

"What do you have?" Alana came to the table at once.

Nancy showed her the notes she'd made, explaining how each one gave her a possible clue.

Alana listened closely, nodding. "So what about the last name?" she asked.

"G. Reed, Cheyenne, Wyoming," Nancy read. "That's a real person. I think I wrote you about visiting there during the Frontier Days Rodeo, didn't I?"

"So what does it mean?"

"*Even four can be hard to handle. Suggest you wait before seeking a newer vehicle.*" Nancy quoted the words, then gasped. "The parade. He must be referring to the parade."

"What about it?" Alana looked confused.

"I was in a runaway stagecoach. I mean, I was riding in a stagecoach and the team was frightened into running away."

Alana just looked at her expectantly.

Nancy stared at the words, sure that she was correct in her interpretation, but unable to see what possible connection there could be between a runaway stagecoach and her father's deadly predicament. "It doesn't make much sense, does it?" she admitted.

"It must mean something," Alana said. "Maybe Ben can help us."

"Ben?" Nancy was surprised at the suggestion.

"Well, if the rest of your deciphering is correct, your father and the Tundra are being held prisoner on an island somewhere near here," Alana said.

Nancy nodded. "Probably an island with a lighthouse on it."

"Ben is a fisherman and he's been all through this area most of his life. He just might know which island it is."

"That would be wonderful," Nancy exclaimed. "Let's get dressed, then I'll order breakfast for all of us from room service." She grinned. "I, for one, am starving. Thinking always makes me very hungry."

Alana giggled. "I haven't been doing that much thinking, but I could eat the menu."

"Don't," Nancy teased. "Without it, we won't know what to order."

Their good spirits carried them along until there was a loud pounding on the wall. "Let's have it quiet in there," Ben's voice carried through to them. "People will think you're having a party."

"We are," Alana called, "and you're invited."

"Be right over."

Ben joined them quickly, a shy grin on his round face. "It sounds like you're feeling better about things this morning," he told Nancy. "Have you solved the code?"

"Not completely," Nancy admitted, "but I have a lot of clues for you to look at after breakfast."

"Breakfast?" Ben looked disapproving. "We can't go out together."

"No need," Alana told him. "I ordered almost everything on the room-service menu. The kitchen probably thinks there are eight people coming to join us."

"Considering that I'm supposed to be alone in this room, you could be hard on my reputation," Nancy observed with a giggle.

Alana joined in laughing but stopped as someone knocked on the door.

Nancy pointed to the bath and waited until both her guests had hidden themselves behind the closed door. She opened the door to the hall carefully, leaving the safety chain on until she was sure there was no one besides the room-service waiter. The clues her father had given her would do no good if the men who were holding him discovered that Alana was with her now.

By the time they'd demolished the ample portions of food, Nancy's happiness had turned to impatience. She got the list and handed it to Ben, explaining each clue to him. He read them over several times, then shook his head. "I don't know of any island they could be using that has a lighthouse on it," he said.

"What about an island that has something to do with a parade, rodeo, team, horses, the West, a stagecoach," Nancy said.

"Stagecoach," Ben murmured, then his dark eyes began to glow. "Coachman Island. It's not very big, but there is an old mansion on it. Some crazy millionaire settled there for a while, built this big house with a tower that looks like a lighthouse." He gasped. "Nancy, that must be what your father saw."

"You've solved it," Alana cheered. "Oh, Nancy, you really did it."

"With Ben's help," Nancy acknowledged, but she felt none of her friend's elation.

"Is there something wrong, Nancy?" Ben asked.

Nancy shrugged. "Not with what we've discovered," she said. "It's the rest of the clues. If Dad included them, they must have some meaning and we can't go after him and the Tundra until I figure out what he was trying to tell me. That's still a mystery."

16

Final Clues

"What do you want us to do to help, Nancy?" Ben asked, forcing her mind away from the puzzle.

Nancy looked at the two, trying to think logically. "You can't stay here," she said, suddenly realizing the danger. "The kidnappers have been in my room twice already. There's no reason to think they won't come again."

"But where can we go?" Alana asked, plaintively.

Nancy looked to Ben.

"She's right, Alana," he said. "They'll come after you if they find out where you are. Our only hope of getting Mr. Drew and the Tundra back is to keep one step ahead of them."

Nancy nodded regretfully. "Is there anywhere you can hide for the day?" she asked. "We could meet back here tonight and you could use the room again and we could make our plans."

Ben grinned. "How about a nice ride on a fishing boat, Alana?" he asked. "That is, if we can rent a car."

"Good thinking," Nancy said. "They know my car now, so it would be good to have another one."

Ben nodded. "I'll take care of it," he said, then sobered. "I want to go by Firebird Lodge, too, and make sure that everything is all right out there."

"Just be careful," Nancy said.

"How do we keep in touch?" Alana asked. "I mean, if you think this telephone might be bugged, we can't call you."

"There's a telephone booth in the lobby," Nancy said. "I'll be in it at noon and again at five P.M. I wrote down the number when I used it last night, so if you want to reach me, call at those times." She gave them the number.

"Will you be all right, Nancy?" Alana asked.

"I will be if I can figure out the rest of Dad's clues," Nancy told her.

Ben and Alana left soon after, promising to use the fire stairs and to be very careful that they weren't followed when they left the hotel. Once they were gone, Nancy wheeled the room-service table out into the corridor for pickup, then returned to the list of clues.

She stared at them, but nothing came to mind. Frustrated, she replayed the tape, seeking some sort of clue in her father's tone or inflection. There was none. Depressed and miserable, she lay down on the twin bed and closed her eyes.

Wearily, she realized she should go down and call Helen. If they were watching her, she didn't want them to suspect that the lists of numbers were a sham.

Then, for the first time, another question popped into her mind. Why had her father included Helen Haggler's name in the list? She was his only real client at the moment, not a name out of the past.

And why had her father been kidnapped before she had come to Alana's aid? How could the men have known she would be in Victoria seeking Alana; and if they couldn't be sure, why had they kidnapped her father?

"They are connected!" she exclaimed, then raced to the table to read the clues she hadn't understood before.

Just be sure that you don't tell one about the others. Let each one think I'm working exclu-

sively for him or her. That was it. Her father had been kidnapped because he was going to Helen Haggler in connection with her investigation of Investors, Inc. Their using his abduction as a threat to force her to find Alana had come later after they'd found out from Nancy's call to Tod that she was looking for Alana.

"You didn't get your tongue twisted, did you, Dad?" Nancy murmured. "My ACB's are the C-B, Inc. investigations and I'd be willing to bet that C-B stands for Cole-Borge."

Feeling lighter by the moment, Nancy picked up all her notes and put them in her pocket, then took her purse and went down to use the phone booth in the lobby. She placed a call to Helen Haggler.

"Do you have any news, Nancy?" Helen asked as soon as Nancy identified herself. "Has Carson been freed yet?"

Nancy bit at her lip, remembering the warning about not telling one about the other. "No, he hasn't, Miss Haggler," she began, suddenly unsure about what she should do. "That's why I called you."

"Do you need help raising the ransom?" Miss Haggler asked. "I can send someone up with cash, if that's the problem."

"They don't want money," Nancy said. "They want someone else in exchange."

"Me?" Miss Haggler didn't sound particularly surprised.

"No, it's the girl I came up here to help," Nancy replied. "I'm calling to ask for more time. I have new information, including a good idea where Dad is being held; but I can't free him before tonight. If you call in the police, we may not have a chance."

"Are you still trying to tell me this abduction has nothing to do with the attempt to take over my company?" Miss Haggler snapped.

"No. When I told you that last night, I didn't know there was a connection, but now I'm sure there is. That's why I'm so positive that Dad is in terrible danger. They can't let him go, Miss Haggler. He knows far too much."

"Then why not call in the police or the Canadian authorities? If you don't think you can ransom him, why wait?"

"If I'm right, we just might be able to trick the men who are holding him."

"You think you can handle it better than the police?" She sounded skeptical.

"Much better," Nancy said. "The men holding Dad want my friend so badly, they'll do almost anything to get her."

"How long do you want me to wait?"

"Until you hear from me?" Nancy suggested.

"Forty-eight hours. If I don't hear from you

before this time day after tomorrow, I'll call the police. Who do I send them after?"

"I'd rather not make any accusations," Nancy began.

"That's the price of time," Miss Haggler said. "If you disappear, too, I want to make sure we know where to start looking."

Nancy swallowed hard. "Do the names Jasper Cole and Felix Borge mean anything to you?" she asked.

"Those two-bit hustlers are behind this? They wouldn't know what to do with Haggler International Imports if they had it."

"If you had a large collection of native art that wasn't yours but wasn't exactly stolen, could you sell it through your shops?" Nancy asked.

"Not honestly, but it would be possible, I suppose," Helen Haggler admitted. "Why? Do they have something like that?"

"They're working on getting it," Nancy said.

"You aren't making a lot of sense," Miss Haggler complained. "But I suppose I'll have to trust you, won't I?"

"I hope Dad will be able to explain the whole thing to you by this time tomorrow," Nancy said fervently.

"And if he isn't able to, where do I send the authorities?" she asked.

"I can't tell you," Nancy said, "but I'll put my notes in an envelope and mail them to you to-day. That way if things go wrong, you'll know as much as I do."

"Notes?"

Nancy explained about the tape and its coded message. "If you don't hear from me in forty-eight hours, maybe the police can use it," she said.

"You just be very careful," Miss Haggler warned. "The men trying to take over my company are completely ruthless. I doubt they'll stop at anything to get what they want."

"They've already proved that," Nancy said, chilled by her words. "But I won't stop at anything either—not until I get my father back!"

17

Plotting an Escape

Nancy made several more calls from the pay phone. Contacting Mr. Steele for a report on the progress of the robbery investigation was the first. It made her feel guilty to listen to the worry in his voice when he asked her about Alana, but she couldn't risk telling him anything.

Next, she called the hotel in Seattle to check for messages, then she tried the Firebird Lodge and was pleased when there was an answer. "Is Ben Qinggoq there?" she asked politely.

"I'm sorry, miss, he isn't," the woman answered. "But I do expect I'll be seeing him in the next day or so. Would you like to leave a message?"

"No, thank you, I'm sure he'll be getting in touch with me," Nancy said.

When she left the phone booth, she looked around, trying hard to remember whether any of the people in the lobby had been there last night, but she couldn't. She got a stamped envelope from the desk clerk and addressed it to Helen, but she didn't put the notes in it. Hoping to find a copy machine, she decided to walk to the nearby shopping area.

"We'll just see if anyone is following me," she murmured, stepping briskly into the damp air.

The streets weren't crowded at that hour, but she couldn't spot anyone. She stopped in a small doughnut shop to wait for the stores to open, then wandered through several before buying some items for what lay ahead. Dark jeans for herself and Alana, plus lightweight, dark-colored sweaters to match.

"Just the right dress for the invasion," she told herself, renewing her determination.

After making her purchases, Nancy moved on to a stationery store carrying maps and bought one that included Coachman Island. She also made photocopies of her notes and mailed the envelope. When that was done, she consulted her watch, and seeing that it was almost twelve o'clock, returned to the hotel.

The people in the chairs and on the sofas of the lobby seemed to have changed, but again, she couldn't be sure. Nancy sat near the phone booth for almost half an hour, but it didn't ring.

Frustrated, but not really surprised, Nancy went into the hotel dining room for a quick lunch, then decided to go to her room. There was always the chance, she reminded herself, that the kidnappers would call for a progress report, and she didn't want them to think that she was merely stalling for time.

When Nancy got on the elevator, she found it half filled by a laundry cart apparently abandoned by one of the maids. She peered inside, noting that it contained mostly uniforms for the hotel employees.

Without really planning anything, she bent over the side of the cart and poked around until she located three uniforms that looked as though they would fit her, Alana, and Ben. She slipped them into the bag with her other purchases and left the elevator on her floor.

Nancy was so busy thinking about what she'd done that she had stepped into her room before she realized she wasn't alone. A scream welled up in her throat, but a hand covered her mouth before she could make a sound.

"It's Nancy," Alana gasped.

"I'm sorry," Ben said, releasing her at once.

Nancy blinked, suddenly realizing the room was so dark because the drapes had been drawn over the windows. "How did you get in here?" she asked.

Alana looked guilty. "I got the key at the desk," she said. "I told them my father had the key to my room."

"Why are you here?" Nancy put the chain on the door. "I thought we agreed you wouldn't be safe here."

Alana started to speak, then burst into tears. "I'm not safe anywhere," she wailed.

Nancy went to the girl and threw her arms around her. "What happened?" she demanded, her gaze on Ben's troubled face.

"We did what you said," Ben began, sinking down on the side of the bed. "Went down the stairs and out the back. We got about half a block, maybe a little more, when a car came along."

"It was those men again," Alana choked. "Jasper Cole and Felix Borge. They saw me, Nancy, and they came after us."

"Oh, no," Nancy gasped, feeling sick. "How did you get away?"

"There was an open office building close by," Ben answered. "We went in there and I had Alana hide in a closet while I led them away. They chased me through three different parking garages and one more building before they found out she wasn't just ahead of me." He grinned. "I kept yelling instructions to her."

"Clever," Nancy said.

"Once they found out it was a trick, they gave up the chase," he continued. "They weren't interested in me."

"I came back here," Alana said. "That's when I got the key. It was the only place we could think of before we split up."

"Of course," Nancy said. "You did the right thing, the only thing you could do. I'm just sorry I spent so much time away."

"Have you managed to learn anything?" Ben asked, eyeing her packages curiously.

"A little more," Nancy said. "But nothing that will help us rescue my father and get the Tundra back."

"What are we going to do?" Alana asked. "We can't stay here. They'll be waiting outside for us, I just know they will."

Nancy nodded, aware that Alana was right. "It's just as well that we're all together," she said, "because when we leave here, we won't be able to come back until afterward."

"Afterward?" Alana's voice held a note of apprehension.

"I have to wait until the kidnappers call," Nancy continued. "I have to make arrangements to exchange you for my father sometime tomorrow."

Alana's expression was bleak, but she nodded.

Nancy sighed. "Alana, I'm not going to, I told you that. The thing is, I want them to *think* that I'm cooperating. I'm just doing it to try to buy some time."

"Do you have a plan?" Ben asked.

Nancy gave him a weak grin. "Not really," she admitted, "but I'll be making one."

"So what do we do now?" Alana asked. "Do you think they'll come to this room?"

Nancy looked around nervously, then frowned. "Where is the tape player?" she asked.

Alana and Ben looked around the room just as she had. "Maybe the maid put it away," Alana suggested. "I mean, the room has been made up."

"She didn't move anything else," Nancy protested, opening drawers and generally searching the room. With Ben and Alana helping her, it took only a few moments to be sure that the tape player was gone.

"I suppose it could have been stolen," Ben murmured, but his tone told Nancy that he didn't believe that any more than she did.

"Reclaimed would be more likely," Nancy

said. "After all, it would have been evidence of my father's abduction."

"What will we do?" Alana shivered.

"I think you two should go next door," Nancy said. "You still have the key, don't you, Ben?"

Ben nodded.

"I don't think they'll check that room, even if they come here," Nancy said, then as the two started toward the door, she called them back. "I do have something that might come in handy," she said, opening her sack.

"What in the world?" Alana asked as Nancy produced the wrinkled uniforms.

"Disguises," Nancy said. "I just happened to ride up in the elevator with the laundry. I thought these outfits might help us get out of here without being noticed."

"Good idea," Ben said.

"Now, my only worry is a car. I haven't had a chance to get a new rental one."

"No problem," Ben answered proudly. "After they gave up chasing me, I figured that was my chance to get a car, so I called a mechanic friend of mine and borrowed his pickup. It's old, but it has a brand-new engine. I put it in one of those all-night parking garages."

"Ben, you're wonderful," Nancy said, giving him a hug.

"Only if we aren't caught," Ben replied, suddenly shy. "Come on, Alana." He took his uniform. "Let's get out of here and give Nancy time to make a plan."

"Just pound on the wall if you need me," Nancy told them.

"You pound for us as soon as you hear from Cole and Borge," Alana said, looking around nervously. "I really don't think we should stay here any longer than we have to."

"Neither do I," Nancy agreed.

Ben and Alana left and Nancy opened the drapes, hoping the daylight would lift her spirits, but it had little effect. There was no sunlight, and heavy clouds seemed to promise rain before nightfall.

Nancy got out the map of the islands and put it on the table. Rain just might be an advantage.

It was nearly an hour before the telephone rang, startling her so much she nearly tipped her chair over as she ran to answer it. As expected, it was one of the kidnappers calling.

"Well, Miss Drew, what do you have to say for yourself?" he asked, his tone full of anger.

"I've found Alana," Nancy answered as calmly as she could.

"You have?" She was rewarded by the surprise in his voice.

"You shouldn't be so shocked," Nancy snapped. "Your men terrified her, that's why she called me for help."

"Do you have her there with you now?" She could almost hear him plotting.

"Of course not," Nancy replied, too quickly. "But I do know how to get in touch with her."

"Suppose you tell me."

"After I have my father with me," Nancy said, her heart pounding with excitement.

"Oh, no, you don't," the man grated. "You'll get your father when we have Alana Steele in our hands."

"You get Alana Steele in your hands when my father is returned to me," Nancy stated.

There was a long silence and Nancy held her breath, knowing the whole plan depended on what was said next. She heard a sigh. "Where do you want to make the exchange?" he asked. "And when?"

"Tomorrow morning," Nancy said, then hesitated. "But I don't know the area very well. What would be a good place?"

Once again there was no sound from the other end, then the man chuckled nastily. "I'll call you at seven tomorrow morning with the location," he said. A click ended the conversation.

Nancy stared at the phone for a moment, then took a deep breath. It was up to her now—to her and Ben and Alana.

18

Rescue Attempt

Nancy slipped into her maid's uniform, then took a pillowcase from the bed. She put the new jeans and sweaters inside along with her purse and everything else she felt she might need. One last glance around the room told her there was nothing else essential to her plan. Taking a deep breath, she hurried to the room next door.

"We heard the phone," Ben said when he opened the door.

"The kidnappers are going to call me back at seven A.M. tomorrow to set up a place to make the exchange."

"Seven A.M. tomorrow?" Alana murmured.

"By that time I expect to have my father and the Tundra safely back," Nancy said.

"Just how do you plan to do that?" Ben asked, his eyes bright with curiosity.

"Let's get out of here first," Nancy said. "I'll give you the details in the pickup."

"So how do we get out of here?" Alana inquired. "Do you think we can just walk through the lobby in these?" She smoothed her uniform down ineffectually.

"I've been thinking about that," Nancy said. "And I have a better idea."

The two listened closely and within minutes they were all together ont he elevator riding to the hotel basement. From there it proved surprisingly simple to make their way through the laundry room, up the rear stairs into the kitchen, and from there out the delivery door into the alley.

A fine mist greeted them and by the time they'd crossed several streets, they were all dripping wet. "Just what we needed," Alana groaned.

"Maybe it is," Nancy replied as Ben led them into the parking garage. "Ben, could we use your boat for our rescue mission?"

"Of course," he said, "but what are we going to do once we get to Coachman Island? Those men will be armed and they aren't going to give up the Tundra without a fight."

"What about your friends at the Firebird

Lodge, would they help us?" Nancy asked.

"They would do anything to help get the Tundra treasures back," Ben answered. "Most of them are from Seal Bay."

"So where *is* the pickup?" Nancy asked, looking around.

"This way," Ben said, forging ahead of them in the shadowy, echoing area. "Where do you want to go?"

"Do you think we'd be safe at the Firebird Lodge for a few hours?" Nancy asked. "We need to sit down and work out the details of my plan."

"There is only one road into the lodge," Ben said. "We can block it and post a guard who will give us plenty of warning if anyone comes."

"Then let's go out there," Nancy said as the three of them got into the battered red pickup.

The now heavy rain stayed with them as Ben drove out of the city, and the roads were empty behind them every time Nancy looked over her shoulder. The Firebird Lodge was warmly lit and welcoming as they pulled up in front.

Nancy froze as two men came out the front door, but Ben leaped from the pickup with a shout of joy to his friends. In a moment they were inside, near the fire, ready to make their plans.

That night the darkness was like a fog around

them as the two fishing boats slipped away from their moorings and chugged out of the small cove that gave them shelter. Nancy and Alana, clad in their dark jeans and sweaters, crouched in the small cabin while Ben and his friend Jim guided Ben's boat through the rough water.

"This is going to work, isn't it, Nancy?" Alana asked nervously.

"It has to," Nancy answered firmly. "It just has to."

As agreed, the two fishing boats stayed within sight of each other until they neared Coachman Island. At that time Ben cut the running lights on his *Salmon Queen*, the signal to the other boat that the plan was now in operation. It was a simple one.

The *Sea Tiger* would approach the island openly, anchoring within the sheltering arms of the bay. It would fake engine trouble and engage in distracting activities on board to hold the attention of any watchman on the alert. Meanwhile, Ben's boat would run without lights as close as possible to the rougher shoreline farther from the house. Once there, Nancy, Alana, and Ben would use a small boat to land.

Nancy could only pray that the three of them would be able to do what a whole squadron of police could not—surprise the thieves and save her father and the Tundra.

"We're getting close," Ben called down softly from the steering bridge. "Get ready, you two."

Nancy swallowed hard, then straightened her shoulders. The weather was still cooperating. Even squinting against the rain, she could scarcely tell the island from the restless water. It would be nearly impossible to spot the fishing boat from the shore, she hoped.

"Are you sure we can't just anchor and leave the boat?" Jim asked. "I could go with you and help out."

"Too dangerous," Ben told him. "A boat at anchor is easy to spot. I want you to patrol this area, back and forth, and watch for us, Jim. We'll be leaving the island loaded and in a hurry, so be ready to pick us up."

Jim nodded, sighing, obviously not pleased with his assignment.

"If we're not back before dawn, radio for help," Nancy told him quietly. "And thank you, Jim. You're very kind to help us."

"To bring the Tundra back, I would do anything," Jim said.

The ride to shore in the small open boat was a nightmare. The storm had made the water very rough and the darkness was like a heavy hand on all of them. Nancy breathed a sigh of relief as the tough little craft grounded against a small area of sand. They could step once more onto land—even though it meant wading in the cold water as they helped Ben drag the boat ashore.

"Now what?" Alana whispered when the boat was safely hidden in some rocks.

"Can you guide us to the house, Ben?" Nancy asked.

He nodded and in a moment they were moving swiftly from the exposed shore into the deeper darkness of the forested island. After several false starts, Ben located a path through the trees and they followed it with ease, not stopping until they reached the edge of a clearing.

"That's the hosue I told you about," Ben said.

Nancy gulped, suddenly very unsure of success. Ben had been right to call the building a mansion. It reared three stories high, with the lighthouse tower rising another two stories to give a commanding view of the area. Only a few windows showed light, but even as they caught their breath, a door slammed at the front of the hosue and two men came out to the exposed end of the verandah.

"I say we wait and watch from inside," one man said.

"And I say you go and investigate while I watch," the second man argued.

"The second man is Felix Borge," Alana

152

whispered. "I don't know who the first one is though."

"Borge was the man I talked to on the telephone," Nancy said.

"Boss, I really think it's just a fisherman caught out in the storm and taking shelter," the first man said.

"Go down to the boathouse and watch them. If they show any sign of trying to come ashore, stop them," Borge ordered. "I'll go in and make sure that Jasper and Drew are quiet, then I'll get back up to the tower and keep an eye on the island from there."

"You can see everything that happens from up there," the man muttered.

"But I'm too far away to act quickly," Borge snapped.

"I'm going, I'm going," the man said.

Nancy closed her eyes, checking her developing plan, then she took a deep breath. "Ben, can you get to the boathouse and put that guard out of commission without rousing the house?" she whispered.

Ben grinned, his white teeth showing in the darkness. "No problem," he said.

"Well, while you're doing that, Alana and I will cross the open area to the house and try to get inside. We'll have to get to the house while

Borge is climbing to the tower or he'll be able to see us."

"What about other guards?" Ben asked.

"If I've read my father's message correctly, there are just three men on the island, so if Borge stays in the tower, Alana and I will just have to get past Cole."

"I'll come to the house as soon as I take care of the guard at the boathouse," Ben promised.

"Won't Borge see you?" Alana asked.

"From the tower, Borge will probably just think it's his man returning," Ben responded.

Nancy nodded her agreement, then gave his hand a quick squeeze as they heard the front door slam again. "Good luck," she whispered. Then she took Alana's cold fingers in her own and the two of them ran lightly across the soaking grass to hide in the deep shadows of the house. They had to make their rescue attempt now!

19

Moment of Truth

The darkness of the shadows that surrounded the building made them feel safe, and as soon as they caught their breath, Nancy began moving along the wall, peering into the lower windows. There was little to see at first. The rooms were dark, but the faint light from the hall showed them to be empty of furniture.

Nancy tried each window and door as they reached it, but they were all locked. "Now what?" she murmured, pausing at the corner of the verandah.

By now, the storm had grown even worse. The wind tore at them as they climbed the steps to the porch. Nancy made her way to the front door and tried it as she had the others. To her surprise, it gave under her touch.

Nancy hesitated, not sure what to do. They had to get inside, but not knowing what was on the other side of the door made it a terrible risk.

Suddenly another gust of wind-driven rain came splattering around the corner of the house and caught the door, jerking it from Nancy's grasp and slamming it against the wall with a sound like a thunderclap. For a heartbeat, Nancy stood frozen, then she grabbed Alana's hand and dragged her through the handsome entry and into the first dark doorway she saw.

"What was that? The voice was Borge's as he came hurrying down the beautiful spiral staircase that rose between the hall and the entry of the house. In a moment, he had the door and was pushing it closed, shutting out the damp scents of the night.

"What's going on?" a second voice asked, as a man came along the hall from the rear of the house.

"I guess the wind caught the door and blew it open," Borge answered.

"You're sure that's all it was? No one got in?" The man sounded more nervous than Borge.

"Look, Jasper, calm down. We'll get the Steele girl tomorrow. She'll tell us the secret of that sculpture and we'll be home free."

"I'll believe it when it happens," Cole said glumly.

"You didn't believe we'd get the sculpture that easily, did you? You keep listening to me, and we'll make your uncle look like the chump he was. He should have left you the sculpture; we worked hard for him."

"He didn't want me to have it," Cole whined. "And neither did that woman he married."

"So we stole it before she could sell it to some place with better security," Borge gloated, "and she won't get near what it's worth from the insurance. We're smarter than the old man ever was and tomorrow we'll prove it."

"If the men from the boat don't get us," Cole said. "Are you sure we're safe here?"

"I've been watching the boat in the harbor ever since it dropped anchor and they aren't even trying to come ashore. You keep an eye on Drew and I'll get up into the tower and doublecheck the area. Bascomb is down at the boathouse watching, too."

"Did you lock the front door?" Cole asked. He was a much smaller man than Felix Borge and he had the look of a nervous weasel.

"If I did, how would Bascomb get in?" Borge asked, not bothering to hide his contempt. "Do you think we have ghosts?"

"Felix, I don't . . ."

"Just relax and quit worrying about every little noise."

The smaller man looked as though he'd like to argue, but a cold glare from Borge kept him from speaking. After a moment Cole turned and disappeared back the way he'd come. Borge grunted, checked the door again, then headed upstairs. Nancy exhaled slowly and felt Alana slump against her in echoing relief.

"Now what do we do?" Alana whispered.

"First we're going to explore a little," the girl detective replied, moving purposefully out into the shadowy entry.

Their explorations were hasty, but thorough. The empty rooms stretched on both sides of the hall and several had connecting doors as well as their openings into entry or hall. The only rooms that appeared to be in use were the ones at the far end of the hall. The kitchen was there and they could see food on the table and dirty paper plates stacked about the cupboards. Since there was a light burning in the room, they hesitated about entering, afraid of being seen through the windows.

Light also showed beneath the door next to the kitchen and Nancy stood there for several minutes, somehow sure her father must be beyond it. Finally, however, she moved away from the door to the dark safety of the room across the hall.

"Well," Alana said, "do you have a plan, Nancy?"

Nancy nodded. "I'm going into the kitchen to get that butcher knife off the table; you can wait in here while I do that. When I'm back, I want you to go to the front of the hosue and open the door we came in so the wind will catch it again. That should bring Cole out of the room and give me a chance to free my father."

"But . . ." Alana gasped, fear in her voice.

"Cole knows who you are, doesn't he?" Nancy interrupted.

"Of course, we met several times before the robbery."

"Well, as long as he thinks you can solve the secret of the Tundra, he's not going to hurt you. But he doesn't even need to see you. You can open the door, then get away through the connecting doors before he comes out. Just keep him busy as long as you can."

"What about Borge?"

"He shouldn't be able to hear anything from the tower," nancy said, hoping she was right. "But if he does, he'll probably just think it's the guard coming back."

Alana seemed ready to debate, but Nancy just gave her a quick, confident grin, then crouched down and half-crawled across the lighted kitchen to get the knife from the table. Alana eyed it warily when she returned to the room.

"I'll need this to cut Dad free if he's tied," Nancy explained. "We have to move fast."

Alana nodded and tried a rather weak smile of her own before she left Nancy's side and started for the front of the mansion once again. Nancy moved back from the doorway of the room and waited, wishing there was furniture to hide behind.

The wait seemed endless and she was beginning to think something had gone wrong, when the whole structure moaned under the attack of the wind and the door crashed open. For a moment there was an eerie silence, then another crash as the wind continued its assault on the door. Nancy braced herself.

The door across the hall opened and Cole came out, complaining angrily. She held her breath as he looked around, then started up the hall. Nancy waited until Cole passed the base of the staircase, then she ran on her toes across the hall and into the well-lighted room.

"Dad!" she gasped as she spotted the bound figure on the straight chair near the fireplace. His eyes lit with delight, but she stopped him from speaking with a finger to her lips, then cut him free.

"Are you alone, Nancy?" he whispered.

Nancy shook her head. "Alana lured him out of here and our friend Ben is on the beach taking care of the guard. Borge is in the tower."

Her father nodded, then moved to stand by the door. He signaled to Nancy to stand behind him out of sight. In a moment they heard the sound of approaching footsteps.

"Have to lock up," Cole muttered to himself. "Can't have the door banging open all the time. Someone might be out there ready to come in." The figure had entered the room first and the hard karate blow to the back of his head ended his words in a muffle.

"I'll tie him up," Mr. Drew said.

Within minutes Cole was bound and gagged and resting in the chair that Carson Drew had so recently occupied. Once that was done, Nancy went into the hall and called Alana out of hiding, then hurried to unlock the front door. Ben came in almost immediately.

"Are you all right?" he asked, frowning. "I saw the door open and there was a mean-looking man silhouetted against the light."

"We're okay," Nancy said, motioning him to follow her. "Did you get rid of the guard?"

"He's tied up and resting peacefully in the bottom of their boat," Ben answered with a pleased grin.

"Come and meet my dad," Nancy said.

Ben's relieved chuckle seemed to fill the entire hall. "What about Borge and Cole?" he asked.

"Cole's also tied up at the moment," Nancy told him with a grin, "but Borge is still in the tower."

"We'll have to do something about him before we can leave," Ben warned. "He's sure to see us and try to stop us."

"Don't worry," Carson Drew said, emerging from the room. "I have no itention of leaving that man running around loose."

Nancy finished the introductions, trying to explain a little about Ben's connection to the Tundra. But before she could say more than a few words, they all heard the sound of descending footsteps.

"Go to the front door, Alana," Nancy whispered urgently, then ran to hide in the shadows under the open-sided spiral staircase, now shaking with Borge's weight.

Nancy looked across the entry to where Alana stood, looking terrified, just inside the door. Borge came around another curve of the staircase, this one just above Nancy, then stopped as he caught sight of Alana. She looked like a mouse trapped in the hypnotic stare of a hungry cat.

"Alana Steele!" Borge's tone was full of wonder. "Where in the world . . ." He started down the last few steps, his eyes on Alana. Nancy thrust her hands through the wide bars of the banister and caught his ankle. He fell heavily, and Ben and her father leaped out to tie him down.

"Where's the Tundra?" Ben asked as soon as Borge was tied up beside his partner.

"Over there," Carson Drew said, indicating a handsome trunk. "That's the protective carrying case Franklin Cole had designed for it."

"Is there anything else we should take care of, Dad?" Nancy asked.

"I think we should get out of here," Mr. Drew said. "These three are not alone in this venture. They have at least two more men out there and when they radio the island and don't get any answer, they'll be coming to their rescue." He looked at Ben. "We do have a way off this island, don't we?" he asked.

"My fishing boat is waiting," Ben replied, "and we can use the radio on it to call in the authorities to pick up the thieves."

"You've done well, Nancy," Carson Drew said, hugging his daughter, "you and your good friends."

"You gave us the coded clues to follow,"

Nancy replied, happy tears filling her eyes.

"Nancy, come and see," Alana called from across the room. "They didn't hurt it at all."

Nancy and her father joined Ben and Alana as they bent over the open trunk, and she caught her breath in delight at the great beauty of the piece of sculpture that rested in its protective nest of padded cloth and carefully fitted restraints. "It's even more beautiful than I imagined," she murmured.

"It *is* a masterpiece," Ben agreed, slowly lifting his gaze from the perfect creation. "It's like a piece of history to me, to my people."

"It's magnificent," Mr. Drew agreed, "but it won't be safe if we don't get it off this island."

"Right," Ben agreed, closing the trunk. "I just hope your daughter does as well at deciphering the secrets hidden in this work of art as she did at finding the clues in your message. What do you think, Nancy?"

"I'll do my best," Nancy promised. "I just hope it will be enough."

20

Tundra Treasure

The next few hours passed as though driven by a kind of whirlwind. As soon as they were on Ben's boat, Nancy and her father had some time to talk. "What exactly happened, Dad?" Nancy asked.

"Well, we were right about Investors, Inc. being a front and you were on the correct trail with C-B, Inc. That was Cole-Borge's corporation and they were the masterminds behind the attempt to discredit and buy out Helen."

Nancy nodded, not surprised. "But how did they happen to kidnap you?" she asked.

"According to what I overheard, Borge called one of Helen's board members and pretended to have information to tell about the fraud. The man told him to contact me and mentioned I was to be at the Haggler estate that morning.

Borge called in two of his cronies to kidnap me."

"You're certainly going to have a lot to tell the authorities when we reach shore," Nancy commented.

"I can give them all the details about what happened to Helen and Haggler Imports," her father agreed. "Cole and Borge talked quite openly in front of me—that's why I was sure they had no intention of turning me loose."

"Why did they want Haggler Imports?" Nancy asked. "Was it so they could sell the Tundra treasures there?"

Her father nodded. "You've worked it all out brilliantly, Nancy. You solved both cases *and* saved the Tundra."

Many hours later the authorities echoed those words to Nancy after everyone had explained their stories a million times. Alana and her uncle Clement were questioned and cleared, as was Tod, since they'd all been forced to cooperate with the thieves by the threats against Alana.

Jasper Cole, Felix Borge, and their guard were brought in from Coachman Island. The other two they'd hired were rounded up and admitted having kidnapped Carson Drew. They also admitted to their part in the plot of terror against Haggler International Imports.

Jeff Carrington came forward to help ease the situation. As an art theft expert who'd worked often with Nancy and her father, his testimony was helpful, along with Helen Haggler's.

Finally, as the afternoon sun broke through the rain clouds, Nancy, Alana, and Ben were allowed to go to the Steele Gallery to see the Tundra. It was a magnificent sight, freed from the protective trunk, each individual carving open to their eyes.

Ben walked around and around it, bending to study first one carving, then another. Stepping back to take in the entire effect, then moving close again to look at something else. Nancy and Alana stayed back, not wanting to interrupt his concentration. Finally, however, he turned and shook his head.

"Nothing," he announced sadly. "I mean, it's beautiful and I feel a great sense of family pride just knowing that my grandfather created it, but I can't find any message."

"Don't you recognize the scene?" Alana asked.

He shook his head. "It's the tundra, Alana. It could be in any section of that frozen land. Unless there's one special rock formation or something." He moved back to study the driftwood and the dried plants and bits of rock that had been placed in the gnarled wood.

167

"Didn't you say that your grandfather left you a message?" Nancy asked.

Ben nodded. "He told the elders of the village to give it to me."

"What was it?"

" 'Look with the eyes of the past to find the darkest dawn,' " Ben intoned.

Nancy waited a moment, then realized he wasn't going to say more. "That's it?" she asked.

His sigh echoed her feeling of disappointment.

"That's not much to work with," Alana observed. "What do you think it means, Nancy?"

"There weren't any other instructions, Ben? He didn't tell his people anything else?"

"Grandfather called in the village elders after the doctor told him he'd never rise from his bed. He said he was sorry he'd deprived the village for so long, but now he was too old and sick to go after the treasures he'd hidden."

"That must mean it would be a long journey from Seal Bay," Alana murmured.

"Maybe," Ben said. "Anyway, the elders told him they would go and get the treasures, but he said they couldn't, that he couldn't even show them where they were hidden without the Tundra. He was very sorry."

"How awful," Nancy said.

"They begged him to tell them what to do,

and he finally said they must find me and give me those words. With them and the Tundra, I would find the treasures for them and for myself."

"And those were the exact words." It wasn't really a question that Nancy asked.

"The elders wrote them down as he spoke them," Ben confirmed.

"Then the secret must be hidden here," Nancy said, moving to the beautiful carving. "But where to look?"

"With the eyes of the past," Alana teased wryly. "At least according to Ben's grandfather."

"The past," Nancy mused. "Something you must have seen then, right? Did you ever go out into the tundra with your grandfather, Ben? Was there a special place?"

"Several," Ben answered. "I spent a lot of time with my grandfather until I had to leave the village to go to high school. My father was always busy working, but my grandfather wanted me to grow up as a proper Eskimo boy, so he taught me to fish and to hunt in the old ways."

"Then this could be a creation of some special place," Nancy murmured, feeling a stirring of excitement. "But what is the darkest dawn?"

"That was always my father's favorite comment," Ben said with a smile. "Whenever anything bad happened, he'd say that marked his darkest dawn."

"Did any of those darkest dawns happen while the three of you were on the tundra?" Nancy asked.

Ben considered, then shook his head. "I can't remember any. I mean, my father used to tell about one time when he was a young boy. He and Grandfather were trailing a herd of caribou near Owl Rock. They were getting meat and hides for the next winter. My father had fallen the day before and injured his ankle, so he couldn't hunt. Grandfather left my father at their camp asleep that morning."

He paused and Nancy held her breath waiting for him to go on.

"Father said it was his darkest dawn because when he finally awoke, he looked up and he couldn't even see the sky because there was a huge grizzly bear coming at him." Ben stopped, frowning.

"What happened?" Nancy asked, caught up in the story.

"Grandfather came and killed the grizzly. I slept under the warm robe they made form it for years. We used to go to that area every year to watch the caribou even after we no longer wanted to hunt them."

"Ben, that's on the Tundra," Alana gasped.

"What is?" Nancy asked.

"The bear and the boy." Alana moved closer to the complex sculpture. "I'm sure I noticed it when I was cataloging the individual carvings. I thought it was sort of scary, the little boy crouched down holding his ankle while the bear stood over him ready to attack." She pointed to the small tableau that was set slightly off to the side of the caribou herd, almost lost in the profusion of dried plants and rocks.

Nancy stared at the tiny figures, then let her gaze wander just a little way beyond them to where another figure crouched, a man's figure holding a tiny owl in his hands. "Is this your grandfather, Ben?" she asked.

When there was no answer, she looked up from the artwork and saw that Ben's eyes were on the carvings and a brilliant smile was spreading across his features. "That's it!" he shouted. "Nancy! Alana! That's the answer! I know where the treasure is."

"Then go," Nancy said. "Don't tell anyone. Just go and get the treasures and bring them back safely before someone else guesses what you are doing."

"Nancy, do you mean other people besides Cole and Borge might be interested in the treasures?" Alana replied.

"A lot of people will realize the legend is true once the details of this case get into the papers and on the news," Nancy reminded her. "It was a lure strong enough to keep Franklin Cole captivated for years and to drive Jasper and Felix to evil deeds. There are bound to be other people just as greedy."

"Thank you," Ben said, his eyes giving the simple words a much deeper meaning. "You'll be the first outsiders to see them." Then he was gone.

"What are we going to tell the police?" Alana asked after a few minutes. "They're going to want to question all of us again, you know."

"The truth," Nancy said. "That he looked at the Tundra and was so inspired he just ran out of the room without telling us where he was going."

Alana laughed. "I just hope they believe us."

"Jeff Carrington will," Nancy assured her.

It wasn't quite as easy as Nancy had hoped, but with the support of her father, Jeff Carrington, Clement Steele and even the reknowned Helen Haggler, the authorities were finally convinced they should wait for the young Eskimo to return. Still, as the days passed and the various aspects of the case against Cole, Borge, and their associates were settled, Nancy worried a little about Ben, alone somewhere on the tundra.

Then on Friday afternoon, Alana called and invited Nancy, her father, and Helen Haggler to dinner at the Steele mansion. "But first come to the gallery," she told Nancy. "The exhibit is finally ready and I want you three to be the first to see it."

As they walked up the steps of the Steele Gallery, Nancy felt a sudden premonition of joy. When the doors were opened for them, she read the truth in Alana's dancing grey eyes. "He's come back, hasn't he?" Nancy asked.

Alana said nothing, leading them into the main room, which was in darkness. As they stood in the doorway, she touched a switch and suddenly hundreds of carvings were lit to glowing ivory life. Every creature of the north was there, every spirit close to the Eskimo heart. The Eskimo people were there in loving detail, a whole record of a village and its inhabitants bloomed from every shelf and pedestal.

"Meet my people, Nancy," Ben said.

"Your grandfather hid all this away?" Nancy gasped.

"He hid the treasures of the village, then added to them through the years. That's why he never showed anything. I think he was punish-

173

ing himself, too, yet he couldn't stop creating his carvings. So he just took his treasures to be with those of his friends and ancestors."

"It's the most magnificent collection I've ever seen," Helen breathed. "I'm so glad you found them and are returning them to your people, Ben. The world will be richer for this inheritance."

"So will Ben's people," Alana said. "The fees from the shows will start to rebuild all that Franklin Cole destroyed."

"Thank Nancy, too," Ben said, "and Alana. They helped me discover the Eskimo's secret."

Hearing Ben's words made Nancy wonder if her next mystery would lead to such an exotic discovery. She would find out very soon.

"You are all honored guests at dinner tonight," Clement Steele announced, interrupting Nancy's thoughts. "The dinner is a celebration and a thank you from me and from the art world for this richness."

"We have a lot to be grateful for," Mr. Drew chimed in. He put his arm around his daughter's shoulders and smiled at her. "This is a happy occasion for more than one reason."

"You're so right, Dad," Nancy said, beaming back at him. "We recovered our own family treasure!"